To Debs
Enjoy
love.
Nergish
(x)

Making Changes

an anthology

Bridge House

British Library Cataloguing in Publication Data

A Record of this Publication is available from the British
Library

ISBN 978-09557910-5-5

This edition published 2008 by Bridge House Publishing
Southampton, England

Contents

Introduction 6
Jigsaw.. 9
Ramani's Eyes 23
The Croc at Coopers Rock 32
I Borrowed a Poltergeist................................ 40
It's a Wonderful Life...................................... 48
Tricks of Firelight 59
Midge and the Pony 66
Winter Blooms... 73
On the Feast of Stephen 83
Dancing Man 96
Moving Magic 109
Choices.. 116
The Keeper's Keeper.................................... 123
Slight Expectations 131
Please, Don't Call Me Herbie...................... 140
Toast and Jam 147
The Blue List 161
Murder in the Air 168
First Impressions... 183
No Smoking Please 194
Sally and the Sign People............................ 204
A Present for St Nicolas 219
Before Twilight.. 226
Mantek's Journey... 234
Index of Authors.. 244

Introduction

The original concept for 'Making Changes' was of an Advent Calendar of stories – one for each day from the 1st of December to the 24th. However, whilst these stories do suit perfectly that delicious time of the year when we can shut out the dark nights and curl up by a fire with a good book, they are relevant for any time of the year. They celebrate life and all that is precious about it.

We start off with Debz Hobbs-Wyatt's intriguing *Jigsaw.* The reader has to work a little on this one to figure out exactly what has happened here. Whatever we decide, it leaves us with a pleasant thrill down our spine.

Oscar Peebles, in *Toast and Jam,* brings us more mystical magic with a touch of humour. There is gentler magic in Nurgish Watkins' *Moving Magic* and in Sarah Harris' *A Present for St Nicholas.*

The latter two are suitable for younger readers, as is Rosemary Gemmell's *Midge and the Pony,* though these three will also delight adult readers.

We touch on the Christmas story with Sally Angell's *Ramani's Eyes,* my own *Mantek's Journey* and Jenny Roberson's *Tricks of Firelight* though all three are unusual enough to intrigue anyone, even those who are not Christian, at any time of the year.

We have stories which give us cause to feel optimistic about human nature in Linda Lewis' *It's a Wonderful Life, Please, Don't Call Me Herbie, The Blue List,* and *First Impressions,* in Rebecca Holmes' *Winter Blooms,* Noreen Wainwright's *Choices,* Wendy Busby's *No Smoking Please* and Jean Lyon's *Before Twilight.* Linda Lewis, in two of her stories cleverly gives us a new take on two stories we know from films – you may recognise references to them in Linda's titles.

6

An anthology produced at Christmas-time would not be complete without a good ghost story and we have three very different and very convincing ones in A.J. Humphrey's *I Borrowed a Poltergeist,* Joyce Hicks' *The Keeper's Keeper* and Michael O'Connor's *Slight Expectations.*

A darker side and therefore some balance is brought to us in Yvonne Walus' *Murder in the Air.* A murder is indeed committed. But will she get away with it? Do we want her to? We are certainly kept intrigued right until the last minute.

Four stories have been included simply because the writing is so strong and evocative that they are a pure joy to read. Ian Charles Douglas brings us psychological tension and a real sense of place in the Australian bush in his *Cooper's Croc.* Pamela Pottinger's *On the Feast of Stephen* seems like a piece of creative non-fiction, a piece of autobiography and we really empathise with the young girl who has to leave her home. Philip Dean Thomas' *Dancing Man* has a strong voice and we have to ask ourselves are we really any different from the stressed journalist or even the dancing man himself, so convinced are we that Graham is a real person. An anthropomorphic main character and a seagull at that is an unusual choice for a Young Adult short story. Yet Rosemary Bach-Holzer's *Sally and the Sign People* is up there with Richard Adams' *Watership Down* and Johanna Reicheis' *Wolf-saga* . I would challenge anyone not to be enchanted by the convincing teenage voice of Sally Seagull.

We hope you will enjoy this collection. I have certainly enjoyed putting it together. The authors featured in this book are enthusiastic, talented, industrious and a pleasure to work with.

If you do enjoy it, look out for our next publication,

this time next year. There will be twelve longer stories –
one for each day of Christmas, but again they will be suitable for any time of the year.

Gill James

Jigsaw

I'm not like other kids. Mum says it all the time when she thinks I'm not listening. She says it isn't normal for people to disappear.

But for me it is.

It's a chronological disorder. They call it lots of different things. Gran calls it *The Gift*. I catch her looking at me sometimes like she thinks if she stares long enough something will happen. Perhaps she thinks I'll become pixellated like when the satellite TV goes weird and that I'll vanish. But it doesn't work that way. I never totally disappear.

Sometimes they call it 'episodes' and sometimes they call it 'spells' but wizards make spells which means something magic and enchanted and it isn't like that. I call it travelling.

I don't know when it's going to happen and I can't control it. It starts with the smell of burning which is weird, given what happened, and it feels like I'm gone for hours but really it's only seconds. I suppose it's a bit like finding a land at the back of the wardrobe.

My name is Leonardo Renoir Hope and I am a seven year old traveller. Hope means "to long for." The thing I long for is to finish the jigsaw I started with my dad that day. He said, "We'll finish it tomorrow." But sometimes tomorrow doesn't come.

Did you know that there are 60,000 fires in the home every year in Britain and that more than 700 people die?

I keep a book under my pillow. I call it 'Our Book of Facts.' It was my dad's idea. He said I should write down about my travels. He said details are really important and writing it down is a way of remembering. I try to remember my dad's hands, the way they looked when they

9

turned the pages. I imagine my hand fitting into his, like pulling on a warm glove.

And then I think, what if I forget?

I've got to find him. I've got to put things right.

My dad said that the world is about rules. He said there are rules for everything. With jigsaws he always started with the corners. So in a special section of our book, after the bit I call 'My Dictionary,' for all my new words, are 'The Rules.' They are the rules we were trying to figure out about travelling.

I haven't seen Dad since that day but I know he is somewhere because everyone is somewhere.

I saw Grandad after he died. He died in Bognor Regis but he was born in Germany. He was struck by lightning when he was trying to fix the satellite dish.

Rule Number 1: Nothing totally disappears.

So I've been trying to find Dad. I've been thinking if we'd finished the jigsaw would there still have been a fire? That's when I got the idea that if I could change one thing maybe Dad would still be here. But that means I have to figure out what really happened.

I used to think that everybody travels, but they don't. Dad said only special people travel. But if that's true then why didn't he travel? And then sometimes I think maybe he *did* travel, but he's lost his RADAR (which stands for RAdio Detection And Range). If RADAR is made up of radio waves that can bounce off raindrops and travel in space, then why can't it work in heaven?

Did you know the first jigsaw puzzle was made to teach children geography?

I wonder if there's a map of heaven? I wonder if it has streets and a house like ours. I wonder if my dad is waiting there for us.

I know about parallel universes, I just don't know how you get to heaven.

But I know the one place that I will find my dad.

Rule Number 2: You can only travel backwards.

I saw a film once when a man kept re-living the same day over and over again. I think it was so he could get it right, so he could make it perfect. That's what's happening to me. I keep travelling back to that day; to that Saturday. Finishing the jigsaw is my way of making it perfect.

Rule number 3: If you think too much about a time you get stuck there.

Did you know you that most fires happen at night when people are sleeping?

Dad knew about fire. Dad knew about a lot of things. He knew about 'flashovers' too. A flashover is "when everything bursts into flames." I don't know why my dad went back into our house that day. That's one of the things I'm trying to figure out.

It was Dad who told me: "Once you have the corners, you can make the edges."

When I'm going to travel and I smell the burning I think about Dad. I try to remember his face; the way it creased up when he was making a joke and the way he threw his head back when he found something really funny. I press the memory into the air so hard I think I can see it hanging there like when you stare at a light bulb for too long.

Sometimes I think I might run out of tears. I never do.

My sister is only four and she's called Monet; Monet Hope with no middle name. I think my mum ran out of artists' names when she called the rabbits Rembrandt and Picasso. I look at Monet sometimes and I think if anyone's going to forget Dad, it's her.

Mum stayed in her bedroom for a long time after that day. She kept the curtains closed. I think maybe that's *her* way of disappearing. If Dad was here he would know what to do. He would know how to reach her.

But that's just it.

My dad's the one that's dead but it's like my mum is the one who stopped living. The words next to Mum in my dictionary used to be 'pretty' and 'kind' and 'my best friend' (apart from Dad) but I crossed it out and now it says 'sad.' I was going to write in capital letters 'SAD', like that, but that means it's a shout and she never shouts that she's sad- she just is.

I'm like my mum.

I never tell her how my heart feels like it's got a crack down the middle and that every time I cry I think it's going to break apart. People sing songs about 'broken hearts.' I used to think, "That's silly, hearts can't break."

But they can.

After Grandad died Gran came to live with us. She said she loved Grandad. I asked her what 'love' means. She said, "This," and she hugged me. Then she said, "Love feels like coming home."

Mum blames Gran for what happened but it was an accident. That means "something that happens by chance." She forgot to turn off the gas after she made co-coa and left a tea towel too close to the flames. That's because she's very old and she forgets things. Mum said the word for it is 'senile.'

But next to the word Gran in my dictionary I didn't write senile. I wrote 'sorry.' And I wrote 'funny' and 'used to be young.' That's because one word can mean lots of things.

My grandad used to be young. He was a soldier. I

saw him a lot when I first started to travel. I told him who I was and he told me lots of things- that's when Dad said I should write them down.

Did you know there were 400,000 German soldiers in Britain after the Second World War?

Grandad said, "Tell me what's going to happen in the future?" He spoke in a funny accent. He clicked his letters as he spoke. I didn't answer him.

Rule Number 4: You mustn't tell.

So I asked Grandad to tell me about Gran. He said he loved her on the day he met her. When I asked *him* what love means he said, "It's a warm feeling that starts in your toes and spreads all the way up to your smile."

I saw Dad when he was young too. I saw him twice. The first time was at The Tate Gallery in London. He was supposed to meet a girl there but she never showed up. I watched him on the steps. Then he asked another girl what time it was. When she turned around I thought my heart would burst through my chest. It was my mum.

Later I asked Dad if I would still be here if the other girl had shown up. I asked him what would have happened if he hadn't met my mum and fallen in love with her. Then I asked *him* what love means. He looked at me for ages, the way he did sometimes when he was really thinking hard about something. I saw his eyes fill up like he was going to cry but he didn't.

Then he said, "When you love someone, Leo, you can't imagine life without them."

"No," I said.

Then he smirked. "The other girl was a scientist. If she was your mum you might be called Einstein or Galileo!"

Then he threw back his head and laughed. I copied him and we laughed so hard we thought we were going to die from it.

When I saw Grandad after he died I hugged him but I think I did it too hard and for too long because there was something odd about his face when he looked back at me. Maybe you can tell people things without telling them? He gave me a photograph and I watched him scribble a message on the back. It was written in German. It said 'Vergissmeinincht.' That means *Forget me not.* I took the photograph back to Gran.

When I asked her about the message she said it's what Grandad said to her on the day they met. Then she cried.

Rule Number 5: It's better not to take things back with you.

There were lots of things that got burned in the fire. I heard Mum talk about insurance. That means 'money that's used to replace things.' But she said there are some things you can't replace. I wonder if she meant Dad. But I still couldn't find him. I *did* find the letters that Dad wrote to Mum when they were at college; ones that talked about love.

Mum said love means "To need someone so much it hurts." I didn't want Mum to hurt. That's why I took the letters for her to find.

Violation Rule Number 5.

Dad said, "Sometimes it's okay to break the rules if it's for the right reason." And I figured that if the reason was to put things right then that was the right reason.

But it just made Mum more sad (SAD).

Rule Number 5 (amended): NEVER take things back.

The other time I saw Dad he was ten years old. He looked

at me for a long time. Then he said, "Don't I know you?"

"You will in the future."

Later I asked Dad about it and he said he never forgot. It's like that with little kids. They always believe.

When they rebuilt our house and painted the living room green, when it should have been magnolia, they found a piece of the jigsaw. The one we never got to finish. The edge was scorched. I tucked it inside the Our Book of Facts. It's like I have a part of him with me. I never told Mum. She doesn't believe. She said she does but I know she thinks that Dad is gone. She says it all the time. I wonder if she remembers his face.

I'd collected lots of facts from that day but I still couldn't figure out what really happened. It's like I had all the pieces spread out on the table but they weren't in the right order.

Dad said, "Once you have all the edges you need to fill in the pieces from the outside."

Dad forgot to put the batteries back into the smoke detector after we burnt toast when Mum was out that time. The alarm kept bleeping for ages even though we waved a tea towel in front of it and stomped our feet like those gay men doing the River Dance. Gay means 'cheerful.' Gran says that Graham Norton off the TV is very cheerful. She likes Graham Norton. He was on TV the day that Grandad got struck by lightning.

Sometimes I lose Dad's face. It breaks up into pixels. That's how I know that time is running out. That's how I knew I had to find a way to travel more; to find the other pieces. So I had this idea…

I did it at night. I tried it with torches at first like the one Mum uses to look inside the smoke detectors that are on the ceiling to see if the batteries haven't leaked. I flashed it really fast right into my eyes. I did it for fifteen minutes. It didn't make me travel but it made me see swirly things in the air and feel like I was going to throw up.

Cool.

So then I decided to switch on the lights in my bedroom really fast: click on, click off, click on, click off, on, off, on, off...

It worked! It *really* worked! The lights would blur into one and then I would smell the burning. The more I did it the more exhausted I was but it didn't matter. I had to do it.

And even thought I still couldn't find Dad I had to start changing things before *he* disappeared.

I decided to put the batteries back in the smoke detector and then when the fire came we would know. But I couldn't reach the smoke detector and I couldn't get back to the day we burned the toast and acted cheerful like Graham Norton to remind Dad to put the batteries back in. That's because, as I said, I was stuck on the day of the fire.

I thought that maybe I could hide the cocoa but Gran would probably have hot milk anyway which means she would still turn on the gas.

And that's when I knew there was only one way: I would have to tell.

(Violation Rule Number 4)

But there was one thing for certain: I absolutely positively MUST NEVER tell ME.

Rule Number 6: NEVER RUN INTO YOURSELF (and that *is* in capital letters because *it is* a shout).

But the thing is... I did.

I had it all figured out, I was going to tell Gran. It would probably make her scream but it didn't matter; she's senile anyway. I would tell her there was going to be a fire and that she mustn't make cocoa. I would say that she had to tell Dad, "DON'T go back in the house." I would write in her hand if I had to.

Then I thought, since Gran forgets things, it would be better to write a letter to Dad that explained everything. But the thing is: THE thing is…I was forgetting about the final rule, the one we were still working on.

Rule Number 7: You CAN'T change things.

Maybe that's why I never travelled for long enough to do any of those things. I never saw Gran, not even long enough to make her scream. I never got to say, "Don't go back in the house, Dad," the way I did over and over into my pillow at night.

I don't know how many times I had to travel by flicking the lights on and off and thinking about Dad before I could finally make out the picture. But I did, in the end…

It was Dad's voice that woke me up that night. I forced my eyes to open but the lids felt heavy, and my eyes were rolling around, slipping to the bottom.

I heard Dad's voice again.

But this time I knew what he was saying. He said, "FIRE!" When I opened my eyes this time they stayed open.

"Get up, Leo," he said and I felt his hands on my shoulders. "Get up!"

The first thing I felt was the heat. It was like when you open the oven door and the heat gushes out onto your face and Mum screams out and says, "Don't stand too close!"

But it was too late.

Dad looked like a ghost, there was a huge blanket over his head and he said, "Come on."

17

I stumbled towards the doorway wondering for a moment if it was terrible nightmare. I squeezed the skin of my arm; pinched it real hard.

But I wasn't dreaming.

When I reached the landing I saw my mum and she was holding onto my sister carefully climbing down the stairs. At each step Mum was feeling the way with her foot and I realised I was holding my breath as I watched them.

There was thick smoke like someone's hand was smothering my face and there was a cracking sound. Maybe that was the sound my heart made when it broke in the middle. Bits of black floated in the air like flapping birds. I felt my hand slide into Dad's and he yanked me forwards. I closed my eyes and willed the world to disappear.

Dad was holding onto me, urging me to follow my mum and my sister down the stairs where the wood was all melted and twisted like the jigsaw on the table in the living room.

Then there was a terrible tearing sound and I felt Dad's hand wrenched out of mine, snapped away from me. I tried to scream but the words got sucked away in the roar. Huge orange flames came up between us. Dad was trapped upstairs; Mum was shouting something from the hallway. I looked back.

"DAD!"

"Keep going, Leo!" he said. "Keep going!"

"But, Dad?"

"I'll climb down the drainpipe... it'll be okay Leo. I promise. Don't look back..."

That's the last thing he said to me. "Don't look back."

So I didn't look back. I didn't. And all the time I was thinking "Dad will climb down the drainpipe and it will

18

all be okay because he promised." I pressed the words
into the hot smoky air until they stuck.

I held my breath and jumped the last three steps los-
ing my footing and it was like the ground came up and hit
my knees. My throat burned, my eyes streamed like I was
crying but I wasn't.

Not yet.

I felt my belly brushing against the floor as I scram-
bled on my elbows.

I kept thinking, where's Dad?

Then I saw it.

I saw the gap where the light came through the front
door and I knew I was going to get out safely. It was going
to be okay.

Or it should have been.

The thing is I couldn't have known it was going to
happen because the warning wouldn't have worked.

There was a piece missing, the one that would show me
why Dad went back into the house. Maybe it was the piece
that got left behind in the box or maybe it was the piece I
had all along. But without it I would never see. And that
meant I couldn't finish the jigsaw.

I still had to travel one more time. And that time I
did see.

I was standing by the table watching as the jigsaw pieces
bubbled and melted from the corners inwards until there
was nothing left. That's when I finally saw. Dad had made
it down the drainpipe and was looking at me. I wanted to
shout, "Go back outside! GO back outside, Dad!" Except
the words wouldn't come, like when you're having a
nightmare, pushing out silent air. Dad was holding something in his arms. My lips fell open. I lifted my hands to

cover my eyes because I didn't want to see. Because the thing in Dad's arms was me. It was the first time I saw what I look like when I travel.

Violation Rule Number 6.

That was the moment that time split like an atom.

Flashover.

Silence.

No one ever survives a flashover. And that means I must have died too.

I open my eyes. There's something rolling between my fingers. I'm in our living room only now it's painted magnolia and not green anymore. The air is cool on my face.

I hear my name being called. I turn around. It's Dad. Oh God, it's Dad! It's Dad! I want to stare at every part of his face, to take it in because I don't know if it's real. I see Monet. She's on the couch and she's staring at me and Mum is reading an art book. I haven't seen her do that since that day.

Dad speaks again. "Well don't you want to finish the puzzle?"

I look at the table with the jigsaw that isn't melted or twisted anymore. I look at Dad's hands.

"What day is it?" I say and Dad looks at me kind of funny.

"Sunday," he says.

It's like that film with the man who wakes up and there's a different song on the radio. It's not Saturday anymore! A scream catches in my throat. I look around the room. But something's wrong. I say, "Where's Gran?"

This time they all turn to look at me like I'm crazy and I think for a second I am.

"At home with Grandad I should think," says Mum and I watch her eyebrows climb into peaks.

"In Bognor?" I say and she lays the book down on her knee and looks at me.

"Where else?" she says.

"He didn't get struck by lightning in Bognor Regis?"

I feel Dad's eyes burning the bit of skin at the back of my neck.

I hear my sister laugh. I look at Dad. He stares for a moment like he's thinking hard, then he throws his head back and laughs. I do too. That's when I finally let go.

"What's up with you!" says Mum shaking her head.

So then I realise: Rule Number 7 (amended): You CAN change things. And I turn to Dad. "You can change things," I say. "You *can* change things. YOU CAN!"

It happened before the flashover; when I was in my Dad's arms. If I was travelling that meant I had to be somewhere else.

I was in Germany and it was a very long time ago. I was standing in front of a little boy.

"I have to tell you something," I said. "But without *really* telling you." I was talking in English but the words came out in German.

Very cool.

I said, "NEVER get satellite." Then I realised he didn't know what satellite was, but he would. "And don't let Gran watch Graham Norton."

He looked at me like I was a total Freak, with a capital F.

Then I remembered something. "Vergissmeinincht," I said.

Then I disappeared.

I look at Mum whose still reading and at Monet who's still staring at me but now she's smiling.

I think, "You don't need RADAR to find your way

back because heaven is anywhere you want it to be."

I look down at my open hand where a piece of jigsaw sits. I scrutinise the edge for a scorch mark and at first I think I can still see it, but then I think I can't.

Our hands touch, me and my dad as we press the last piece into the puzzle. He smiles at me.

My book is open on the table at the dictionary part. Next to the word 'love' I've written 'Dad.'

D A Hobbs-Wyatt

Debz Hobbs-Wyatt lives, breathes and sleeps words! She is currently working on her third novel. She describes her writing as paranormal psychological fiction – with a heart. She is currently seeking an agent with her second novel, 'Colourblind', and dreams of giving up her day job!

Learn more at: http://debzhobbs-wyatt.blogspot.com

Ramani's Eyes

The noise and commotion surprised Ramani as she approached her village. It was usually quiet here in the early afternoon when the bazaar was closed, and people rested or were about their business. Today many were standing outside their houses, and women huddled together wailing.

"What has happened?" Ramani asked one of them, but the woman just cried out as if in pain. As Ramani watched, a man she recognized as the doctor who had birthed her sister came running. The women led him through one of the entrances, and they all disappeared inside.

Ramani was worried. Her family lived in the valley over the rocks, and she wondered if they were in danger. But she did not want to go home. Her mother would be angry with her. Ramani knew what she would say.

"Oh no, Ramani, Ramani. Not trouble at the hostelry, again?"

Ramani thought quickly. Perhaps she could just pass by the house without being seen. She sped through the streets to the small white building where she lived with her mother and father and baby sister, Rebeka. Ramani kept out of sight, hiding by the well, from where she could see through the window arches. Her mother and the servant girl were sitting at the wooden table in the living area, plaiting rushes, and Ramani could just see the top of Rebeka's bright hair. Whatever had happened near the bazaar, Ramani's own family were safe. For now.

"Thank you," Ramani whispered. She could not imagine what she would do without them. But people had been warned for weeks to be alert, as large numbers of strangers poured into the area for the government census.

The dangers might not be over yet.

As always when troubled, Ramani turned her eyes to the hillside behind the village. She hurried across the sandy waste ground to the edge of the springing grasses, and started to climb the track.

Uncle was leaning against a rock half way up the hillside. He didn't seem surprised to see Ramani, and nodded quietly. His flock were roaming, or standing in the sheltered place. The shepherd boys, Aman and Rajive were sitting under a tree.

"Greetings Uncle. Greetings Rajive, Aman."

Ramani knelt down by a small sheep that wasn't standing up.

"Hello, little one," she murmured.

The sheep was black and frizzy and not like the others. Ramani remembered helping with the birthing, back in the spring. She loved to see the tiny creatures fall out and wake up to life, and she never minded the blood and strange smells and the wetness. She had named this lamb Night, fed it with milk and took it home with her to keep it warm. Night had been so weak they didn't think she would live. She was still much smaller than the others. Ramani held out her finger and the little sheep nuzzled it.

"Ramani, will you watch the flock. We are needed down in the village." Uncle looked at her as if not wanting to frighten her. "A babe has died. They need all the men down there."

The pictures flashing before Ramani's eyes made her body shake so that she fell over. She had seen them before. She knew now what had happened. Her mind was filled with fear for her family. Never mind what her mother would say about the Mistress dismissing her from her work in disgrace. Ramani had to go home.

"Can one of the shepherd boys stay with the sheep?"

Ramani asked Uncle. "My mother needs me."

Uncle handed his crook to Rajive and gave him instructions. Then he and Aman set off across the hills. Ramani stumbled back down the hillside. Back within the familiar walls she had known since she was a child, she felt safe. It was cool indoors, and she found comfort in the sights and smells of the house. She could hear the servant girl singing to Rebeka, and smell the aroma of her mother's bread baking in the oven. Her parchments were neatly arranged on the ledges which her father had carved and coated in pale blue dye, for his eldest daughter.

Ramani lifted down a scroll and lost herself in the words. Her mother came in carrying a basket of garments.

"Oh Ramani. Will you stop reading and listen to me. I have just received a message from the keeper of the hostelry. The mistress has reported that you let the pans boil dry again. She cannot trust you to do your tasks." Ramani's mother's face was colourless with tiredness, and fear. Ramani could see her thin arms trembling underneath the basket.

"I have enough to worry about with this new trouble." Ramani's mother lowered her voice so that the servant girl, nearby, would not hear. "A babe's life has been taken in the village. You remember we went to the boy's blessing."

Ramani remembered the celebrations. The parents of the newborn were so happy. A chill ran up her back like a cold hand.

A familiar sleepiness was beginning to creep through Ramani's body. She tried to fight it off through the mists gathering before her eyes, afraid of what she might see. The images persisted and although they were fuzzy, she could see the events that were taking place.

Ramani spoke urgently. "Listen to me, my mother.

There are bad men here. You must not take Rebeka outside the house, and you must guard her even when she sleeps. I don't know why, but I don't think she is in danger. However, you cannot take the risk."

There was a clatter and the snort of horses outside, and Ramani's father entered. He was a merchant who traded in the City. Ramani's mother quickly told him about the tragedy that had befallen the neighbour's child.

Ramani's father nodded, his face serious. "There have been others."

"It is the men I saw," Ramani cried. "Dangerous men. They are from the government." She had seen pictures of these men in her head, a year ago. The men who had been sent to harm infants. No one had believed her and now she knew why. It had been the wrong time.

"Don't start all that nonsense again, daughter," Ramani's mother said sharply.

"Let the girl be." Ramani's father was a quiet man, but when he spoke people listened. "Her grandmother was the same, and my mother's mother. She cannot help what she sees. When she is past the unsettled years and is living the life of a woman, it may pass."

"So many worries. You know we need more ointments for Rebeka, Solam," Ramani's mother said. "We have to pay the alchemist."

Ramani felt an ache of sadness. She knew her father did not earn a great deal of money. He sold the woven goods that Ramani's mother and aunts made and other products. They might just have managed if it wasn't for Rebeka's treatments.

Ramani had wanted to study. She longed to read and learn. She would find herself thinking about all that happened in this land and other lands. Her father said he was sorry but she would have to work and help with the family earnings.

Ramani had tried hard, but she was not good at the laundry and meal preparations, and felt shy and awkward when serving the hostelry guests with ale and food. She longed to sit with the scribes and learn of the secrets of words and stories.

But Ramani loved her sister and could not bear to see her sick.

"I will work harder, mother, at the hostelry if the Mistress will give me another chance." Ramani meant this. She would pay attention to her tasks and learn to become accomplished in skills which did not come easily to her. But there was the other problem, and she was afraid, for she could do nothing about that. She could not stop the pictures when they came. They blotted everything else out while they lasted. The pans would boil over and the irons set on fire.

"Oh Ramani." She felt the warm arms close around her awkwardly. It was unusual for her mother to be demonstrative, for she always had so many cares. "It is true," her mother said. "Your father's mother had beautiful eyes like yours, the colour of the deep blue ocean. And she was a wise woman."

Ramani slept in Rebeka's room that night to watch over her. She stayed awake as long as she could in case any harm should come to her sister.

The Mistress sent another message in the morning, to say that she was giving Ramani another chance. She could go back to her work.

"You are lucky," her mother said. "The keeper will need extra help at this time."

She was right. The hostelry was overflowing with travellers who had arrived for the census in Town. All the inns there, and in the surrounding countryside and villages were full up. People had to journey to the signing centre for their native region.

Every room was taken. Even part of the keeper's private quarters had been furnished with raised wooden slats and bedclothes. Ramani knew because she helped to set out the water jugs and drying cloths. She often stayed late with extra duties.

One evening on her way home, she looked up to the hillside. The sky was casting its darkness like an umbrella, covering the rocks and hills. There was a deep chill in the air. Ramani thought about the sheep in freezing temperatures. She decided to go up to check on them.

It was slippery. Snow sparkled on the ground like sprinkled crystals. When Ramani reached the place where the shelter that Uncle had built in case of weather hazards was, it was deserted. Ramani felt fingers of coldness touch her neck. Where was Uncle? And there was no sign of Aman and Rajive. Uncle loved his sheep like he loved his children. He never left them unattended. The animals were gone, except for a couple of strays roaming.

What was that? She could just make out a soft mewing. Ramani followed the sound and peered through the gloom. The little black lamb, Night, was lying in a crag. Her leg was tucked awkwardly under her. Ramani climbed down and lifted the lamb free.

"It will be all right, little one," she whispered.

Ramani tucked the tiny creature under her robe, and started off through the darkness. She had only white footmarks to see by. She had not gone far when she thought she saw Uncle in the distance. She was about to call out, but something stopped her.

Uncle and the shepherd boys were standing in a circle of light, which was odd because there was no moon. There must be someone else there because Ramani could hear a voice. But she couldn't hear what it said and she couldn't see anybody else there.

The light dimmed and Ramani stumbled over to the place. Uncle looked dazed.

"We're to go to the town," he said. "A boy is born. An important child."

"In a manger!" Aman said, skipping in excitement. "That's where he'll be."

"Would an important child be born in a stable?" Uncle wondered as they kept on walking.

When they reached the town Uncle made enquiries at the houses and inns. Everywhere was crowded. The shepherd boys had a look round any stables but found them crammed full with horses, and stable boys trying to calm and feed and water them. Ramani wished the pictures would come to her to give her guidance. But she had no control over when they would happen.

Ramani, Uncle and the shepherd boys arrived at the hostelry, which was on the edge of Town.

"I will go and look in the stables," Uncle said, and went off with Rajive and Aman.

Ramani was about to follow when a voice rang out.

"Ah Ramani." The Mistress! "We need your help tonight. We are so busy."

The lamb moved under Ramani's cloak. She held her breath, but the Mistress was too harassed to notice anything amiss.

"Go to the kitchens first, girl."

As Ramani passed through the drinking bar, her heart seemed to stop working properly. Some of the guests were the men she had seen in her pictures. Fortunately, they would consider themselves too grand to go into the places the animals were kept, but if a child was birthed anywhere on the premises, they would hear about it.

Rajive came running.

"He is here! You would not believe it. In a manger, near the animals."

"Ssh!" Ramani drew him aside. "Rajive. Hurry and tell the citizens of the town to guard their little ones." He ran off.

Ramani hurried to the kitchens. She stood on a wooden block and reached a jar down from a high ledge. Her heart hurt in her chest, but no one noticed her. They were all too busy, shouting orders, roasting chickens, and stirring sauces. Ramani put sprinkles from the jar in with some breads and sweetmeats on a plate. She picked up the plate with one hand, still keeping the lamb safe with the other. .

Breathing in air very slowly, Ramani went into the drinking bar and walked up to the men and smiled. They laughed and took the food from the plate she offered.

Ramani watched as the men ate and talked and then stumbled over to side seats where their heads began to droop. Ramani knew it was no use telling the officials about these men because they were the king's friends, and no one would believe her. But for the moment, they could do no harm.

Ramani slipped out of the side door of the hostelry, and sped across the dark yard to one of the outbuildings which was lit up. Inside, a donkey was tethered to a stall. A young woman was sitting on a bale of hay. Her smock was shabby, her face red and shiny, and her feet bare and dusty, but she looked beautiful. The man behind her was older. He looked dazed, but was staring at his wife and child in a way that Ramani had seen her father look at her mother and herself and her sister.

Ramani found Uncle and told him why she was worried. The men would only be in a deep sleep for a few hours.

Uncle whispered. "It is all right. The couple are leaving with the babe at first light, to go to a far country." Ramani saw light through the stable entrance and realized it was almost morning. What a night!

From the dark corner of the stable Ramani stared at the little family, and pictures flooded before her eyes, as brilliantly coloured as the illuminated texts on the walls of the temple. Joy swept through Ramani, as the scenes of love and wonderful events and great healings unfolded.

When the pictures stopped, Ramani felt different. She sensed she wouldn't be seeing them again. And that knowledge and learning would come from living her life fully. There would be time for reading and writing and travelling. But that time was not now.

Ramani wanted to tell the girl, "Your son will be greater than you can ever imagine. There will be suffering, but such joy and love after, and change such as the world has never seen." But for now the young mother was happy, smiling and touching the gifts offered to her little son in wonder.

Unnoticed among the noise and people and excitement, Ramani crept to a corner of the stable. She tucked Night into a warm bed of hay, took a last look at the mother and baby, and crept away to carry out her Mistress's orders.

Sally Angell

Sally Angell writes fiction and poetry, for children, and for adults. In her writing she likes to explore the truth and reality of feelings, the originality of language, and the possibilities of words. website: www.sallyangell.firecast.co.uk

The Croc at Coopers Rock

Even upside down the desert was boring. Jana studied the islands of cotton wool.

They were drifting across a bright blue sea. Above them, the endless sands made a reddish sky. The scene shimmered in a heat haze. Pretty, but definitely a yawn. Jana jumped down from the desert oak. Her head felt dizzy, but that passed as her bloodstream flowed back towards her feet. The sky and the ground were back where they belonged. But they were still dull, not to mention hot. The guesthouse garden was roasting under the oppressive sun.

"What ya doing?" The words caught Jana by surprise. She wheeled round. It was the Aboriginal boy, coming down from the guesthouse. Jana had seen him before, running errands for the landlady. Jana's mother didn't approve of her talking to the Aboriginal children. Still, Mum wasn't there now.

"I'm waiting," she said grandly.

"Waiting for what?" the boy asked, scratching his thick mop of hair.

"Waiting for Mum to come back. Waiting to go home to Sydney. Waiting for the world to end. Waiting-"

"Alright. I getcha Missy. Where's your Ma?"

"At the Observatory, she's important." Jana was talking in her queenly voice.

Mum said she had a gift for it.

"Alright, lot of city fellas come out to see the star house."

Jana smirked. Probably he couldn't say *observatory*. Back in Sydney her schoolmates loved telling Aborigine jokes. Mum said you shouldn't laugh at other people. Yet Mum had forbidden her to play with the Outback children, even before they boarded the bus in Sydney. Mum also said the correct term nowadays was "Indigenous Australians," although Mum never used those words with other grown-ups, only with Jana.

The journey to Coopers Cross lasted two days. Mum kept herself busy with her laptop. She looked at maps of the constellations and revised her calculations. But the trip had been extremely tedious for Jana. Hours of driving, watching the green farmlands fizzle out into red soil.

The Outback was another world. Jana understood now what people meant when they said that. Millions of tons of rust-coloured dirt lifted from Mars and scattered as far as the eye could see. Even the plant life appeared alien. Clumps of grass filled the redness with green streaks. Stumpy white gum trees were scattered everywhere. Jana imagined them as skeletons bursting from the earth, as if in a horror movie. But a wilderness was a wilderness, spooky trees or not. There were no fast food restaurants, no cinemas, and no malls. Totally nothing. So it was weird and boring. Jana didn't like that combination.

The boy stood in the shade of a wilting jacaranda tree.

"What ya got red hair for?" he asked casually.

"Scottish ancestry," she explained proudly, as if it made her a millionaire's daughter.

"Aw, right," he replied politely pretending to understand, though Jana knew he didn't. They stared at each other for a moment. Then the boy spoke.

"I'm going to the Rock if you wanna come."

"Rock? What rock?"

"The white fellas call it Coopers Rock. Out of town, about a mile."

Jana screwed up her sea-blue eyes and stared at the boy hard. *The white fellas call it Coopers Rock*. What did that mean?

"Yer, the Rock has a Dreamtime name. But that's secret, Missy!"

Jana said nothing. She knew the Indigenous Australians believed their legends were sacred.

"OK why not, I'll get some water and meet you out front!"

The inside of the house was quiet and cool. The landlady told her guests to treat the place like home. So Jana helped herself to two large bottles of water, and a selection of sandwiches she found in the huge old refrigerator.

On the porch she picked up one of the communal bikes. The boy was waiting on the street, perched on a rickety old cycle. They slowly cycled out of town, heading west. The route led deeper into the banking sands. The boy pointed out Coopers Rock. It looked like a prehistoric termite nest. A series of orange globes stacked up, one on top of the other.

It was too hot to pedal fast. They laughed as they took turns at overtaking. There was plenty of time to talk and Jana learned more about her new friend. His name was Josiah but his nickname was J-Boy. His family was so large he couldn't count how many relatives he had. Mathematics was his favourite subject at school. J-Boy didn't need to ask Jana any questions. She eagerly told him everything she knew about her mother. How Mum was a world famous astronomer at the University of New South Wales.

"Does she know any astronauts, Jana?" J-Boy wanted to know.

"Not really. Mum's more concerned with distant galaxies than space shuttles. That's why we're here. Mum's researching the Big Bang."

"What's that mate? A bomb?"

"It's a very special explosion. The Big Bang created the universe, the beginning of everything"

J-Boy laughed loud as if Jana had said something foolish.

"You city fellas! That's Dreamtime."

"What?"

"The beginning of the world was Dreamtime. There was no bang."

Jana started to explain that the Big Bang was a scientific theory, while Dreamtime was just a myth. But the words died on her lips. What exactly was the difference between a theory and a myth? Out in the fierce heat Jana wasn't too sure.

Close up Coopers Rock was even more peculiar, almost manmade. It was as if a giant had carefully polished some stones, then piled them up on the desert floor.

"'The Big Croc' done Cooper's Rock, back in Dreamtime."

"Sure," Jana replied with a big grin.

J-Boy pointed up to a V shaped cave, where one cliff leaned against another.

"Lot of Dreamtime magic there," he said. "Wanna see?"

Before Jana could answer J-Boy scrambled up over the smaller boulders that made steps to the cave. For a moment Jana contemplated the danger. Just for a moment.

"Wait up!" she hollered and started after him.

The cave was more of a crack, running down between two rock-faces. Peering dubiously into the gloom she spied a triangle of light below. But would she get stuck on the way? No wonder her mother didn't want her talking to the Aboriginal children!

"C'mon, it's easy," J-Boy said, with a big grin.

He disappeared into the hole. "Don't be sissy."

"You might be made of rubber, but I'm not," she replied. But the gibe worked and Jana scrambled in, head first.

Out of the desert sun it was much cooler. J-Boy had vanished. Jana shuffled down the stone gully. Sandstone ridges scratched at her knees. The light seemed to shrink away. The gully tightened. Worse it started to fall.

"Help!" Jana was tumbling.

The next thing she knew the cave spat her out, as though she tasted disgusting. With a nasty bump she landed on a pile of pebbles. Angrily she looked around for J-Boy, with a few rude names in mind. She couldn't see him anywhere, but the sound of giggles stirred through the grass.

What a strange place, Jana thought. A large basin hidden inside Coopers Rock. Was this one of those Aboriginal watering holes? Mum once told her the Outback was sprinkled with secret oases. The native people had used them for centuries. A deep pool filled the basin, like black glass. Yellowy reeds grew all around, with the odd eucalyptus tree struggling upwards. One tree caught her attention. A peculiar writhing ball clung to its trunk, a bee swarm!

J-Boy appeared at the tree, laughing.

"Don't worry Missy. Cooper bees friendly." He reached up, delved into the mass of insects and pulled out a handful of honey. "Delicious," he said, licking his palm.

Jana hopped across three stepping-stones in the pond. She stumbled on the last one, but J-Boy caught her with his clean hand.

"Want some?"

"Why didn't they sting you?"

"Aw, they're sleepy. No worries Miss Jana. Wanna go?"

The afternoon was turning into one dare after another, but Jana was not to be outdone. She lifted her hand to the opening in the trunk. The nest was inside.

"Not too quick, not too slow, alright?" the boy said.

Carefully she pushed her hand deep into the hot buzzing morass. She felt something sticky. Out came her hand, dripping with dark honey. Jana gave J-Boy a triumphant sneer. It tasted sweeter than anything on the supermarket shelves.

"CROCODILE!" J-Boy screamed. For a second she didn't believe him. J-Boy was pointing to the far end of the pool. A huge shape was moving towards them, under the surface.

"RUN!" he shrieked.

In panic Jana slipped off the stepping-stone. She bounded away from the water, into a maze of boulders. A noise of something *slithering* whispered around the cavern walls. Jana's heart iced up in fear.

"Jana, stay there," came J-Boy's voice, trembling. "Big crocodile outside your hiding place."

"There AREN'T any crocs here," Jana stammered, trying to sound brave. Surely the nearest crocodiles were five hundred miles north, in Kakadu.

"This Pikawu, crocodile man in Dreamtime!"

Jana scanned around, but there was no escape. Cliff walls towered above her.

"Pikawu very bad croc. He eat many children. Ancestors kill him with nulla-nulla."

Jana wasn't too sure what a nulla-nulla was, but she wished she had one right now. A stone the size and shape of a rugby ball lay at her feet. Jana heaved it up and hugged it to her chest. Thoughts flapped through her head like frightened birds. Was she strong enough to batter the monstrous reptile and live? No way! Was there really a croc anyway? Could it be another of J-Boy's pranks? But then what had she seen under water? What had made all that scraping and padding?

"Bad Pikawu. Go away. This place safe. Ancestors sleep here." J-Boy was talking to the beast. Ancestor spirits? Real or imaginary Jana prayed for their help.

A sudden inspiration struck.

"J-Boy, where is it now?" she called out.

"Outside your rock, near the honey tree."

Jana let out a terrible grunt and leapt from her hiding place. The creature stood before her in the blinding daylight, a great, scabby, evil-eyed dinosaur. With all her strength Jana threw the rock. It flew right over the crocodile's head, perfectly aimed for quite a different target. The boulder smashed into the bee's nest and exploded into a thousand splinters, small, striped, angry splinters.

"Our very own Big Bang," Jana gasped.

The bees erupted in cascading patterns. They danced ferociously, making furious fireballs in the air, before diving upon the nearest moving object. This was the unfortunate crocodile. Terrified, the poor creature waddled away on its fat legs. The bees flapped after it, like a cape in the breeze.

Only it wasn't a crocodile. No, it was a beautiful, multi-coloured goanna. True, it was unusually large but nowhere near right the size, for even an adolescent croc. This wasn't Pikawu.

J-Boy, who was up a eucalyptus, shrugged his shoulders.

"Pikawu very tricky today," he beamed.

*   *   *

38

The desert felt hotter at night. The sand was releasing the heat it had trapped during the day. Jana sat on the balcony, nursing a bee sting. Mum was inside on the bed, absorbed in her calculations. She turned and gave her daughter a long thoughtful look.

"Are you seeing that boy with the vivid imagination tomorrow?"

"Yes Mum."

"Be careful," Mum said, none too pleased.

Another silence passed and then Jana spoke.

"Why don't you put down those star charts and come and look at the real things!"

"Good idea." Mum said and joined her.

The desert was dark and brooding. The stars shimmered in the heat as brightly as fireflies.

"I'm so glad we came," Jana said.

"Really? I thought the Outback was boring you stupid?"

"Boring?" Jana sounded shocked. "The desert's alive! Everywhere there's something to see. I think there must be as many secrets in the desert as there are up in your stars!"

Jana's Mum laughed.

"Maybe you'll discover a few before we leave?"

Jana looked right back at her and smiled.

"Maybe I will."

Ian C. Douglas

Ian Charles Douglas cut his literary teeth as a freelance writer in East Asia. He returned to the UK to complete his MA in Creative Writing and settled in Nottingham. Ian now focuses on children's fiction with a passion for science fiction. For more information please visit http://www.iancdouglas.co.uk.

I Borrowed a Poltergeist

"Is it just me?" she whispered, "or does it feel as if Christopher Lee is going to come sweeping down that staircase any minute, and invite us upstairs for a bite?"

I could see what she meant. Outside, the hotel had seemed nothing more than a rectangular building on the quiet corner of the square, built of that reddish stone that was in vogue with the builders of Victorian London. A little faded and crumbly with rain and pollution – nothing special. Passing through the revolving door with its burnished brass handles, however, was like stepping into another era. Directly ahead, a magnificent mosaic floor led towards the closed and curtained doorway of what must have been an enormous ballroom. To our right, a passage carpeted in heavy burgundy-coloured pile led to a gloomy mahogany bar. Through the archway to our left, the whole length of a wall was taken up by the most enormous reception desk I have ever seen; and ahead and slightly to the right rose a colossal staircase of garish mottled marble, held up by curling pillars, and with a polished brass banister reflecting the glint of the chandelier high above. It certainly bore all the hallmarks of a place from one of those absurd old horror films I used to watch as a teenager.

A polite cough from somewhere behind my left shoulder made me realise with a start that an elderly gentleman had joined us. He was the concierge, clad in a black tail-coat, and he looked almost as old as the hotel, stooped nearly double and with a long, wizened chin. A genuine hunchback. I wondered if he'd been employed for his looks; whoever owned this hotel clearly had predilections somewhere to the left of gothic. I was half expecting a non-specific Eastern European accent, so was a little taken aback when he opened his mouth and let out a cheerful "Show you to your room, guv?" in perfectly merry Cockney.

He didn't even have to ask us which room it was. Room 545 (the Trevor McDonald Suite, as I'd jokingly nicknamed it) was a short lift journey away, at the end of a quiet corridor. The reception area may have been magnificent, but the upstairs corridor where our room was situated was dusty and just on the wrong side of shabby. The walls were papered with a faded, pale green wallpaper that was fraying and coming adrift in places. The carpet wasn't much better, crying out as it was for a good shampoo and set. Of course, that's the whole reason this hotel had been so cheap in the first place. They were in the middle of renovations, with only a few rooms open to the paying public, at a discount for any inconvenience that the ongoing works might cause.

From our point of view, it didn't matter a jot. The hotel stay was a spur of the moment excursion, hastily arranged the day we heard that one of our old university mates had landed the lead role in a cutting-edge radio comedy, and that he'd invited us to join the studio audience for the recording of the first episode. I'd have been happy with a Travel Inn next to the railway, but Lucy had preferred to go for something with a little more character. A quick trawl of the internet, and the Trevor McDonald Suite had been the result. They weren't wrong; the place had character in spadefuls.

"If this place is practically deserted," I mused as I perched on the end of the bed and pulled off my boots, "how come they stuck us in the smallest room in the place?"

"We only got what we paid for," she replied from through the doorway into the en-suite. "Anyway, what are you complaining about? You could get the court of King

Caractacus in this bathroom!"

Lucy was right. Although the bedroom was small and narrow, dominated by the sturdy double bed on which I was perching, the bathroom – inlaid with black and white mottled marble, with polished brass rails – was little short of palatial. I could almost imagine a movie star of yesteryear, draping herself becomingly in the magnificent stone bath. Lucy was plucking her eyebrows in front of the mirror, possibly aiming for something of that old sophisticated glamour herself. I was now down to bare feet and had abandoned my tie, letting it fall in a heap on the edge of the bed. At least, that's what I *thought* I had done with it. When I looked again, not half a minute later, it was neatly folded and resting on my pillow.

"Don't be too long in there, will you?" I called out lazily, flicking through the welcome brochure. "*Professor Zargov's Laboratory of Lunacy* waits for no man, you know."

"Professor Zargov's not for two hours yet. I've got time for a bath before we head out."

"Barely," I muttered under my breath, as I knew exactly how long it would take Lucy to finish in there.

By the time she emerged, I had mastered the antique remote control and was three-quarters of the way through *Hollyoaks*. "Isn't there anything else on?" she asked breezily, wrapped in a bath towel, as she snatched the device from my lazy hand. "What about VH1?"

Quite how she managed to fling the remote halfway across the room, I have no idea. It left her hand as effortlessly as she had seized it, and clattered heavily into the coffee table. I was worried, for a minute, that we might have damaged something; the device was the weight of your average half-brick, and I didn't relish the prospect of an evening ringing round the *Yellow Pages* for a French polisher to patch up any scratches on the furniture. As it transpired, we were lucky; there was no damage done.

"Did you see that?" exclaimed Lucy, double-checking the smooth dark surface of the table for scratches. "It just flew out of my hand!"

"Maybe the local poltergeist wants to watch the end of *Hollyoaks*." I held out the welcome brochure to her, pretending to show her the list of room features. "All rooms are equipped with en-suite bath and shower, trouser press, tea, coffee and hot and cold running poltergeists. They'll even do Room Service for us if we tip 'em thruppence ha'penny."

I proceeded to make poltergeist jokes all the way along the corridor, down the lift and out across the mosaic tiling into the London night air. *Professor Zargov's Laboratory of Lunacy* trod a satisfying line between inspiration and idiocy. I don't think it was honestly *quite* as cutting-edge as our thespian friend had led us to believe, but it would clearly fill up half an hour on the late side of *A Book at Bedtime* quite splendidly. There was certainly something to be said for being in the front row watching one of my oldest friends make a complete and utter prat of himself.

After a brief post-performance drink with the star of the show, we made our way back to the hotel. For all they say that London never sleeps, it was eerily quiet in the square by the time we returned. A light mist was beginning to curl its way in tendrils around the street lights. I'd always thought that mist with *curling tendrils* was a bit of a cliché, but I can honestly say that that's exactly what the mist was like tonight. It was a Jack the Ripper, Professor Moriarty, Jekyll and Hyde kind of night, and it didn't do to stand still too long, in case the chilly damp crept into one's lungs and caused a cough that would take the whole of next week to dislodge.

"D'you think he's watching us?" I asked as we stared up at the hotel's farthest windows, idly trying to work out which one belonged to room 545.

"Who?"

"The poltergeist. What do you reckon?"

An unexpected transformation had taken place inside the hotel while we were out. The mosaic floor was covered with old white sheets. There was a paint-stained ladder propped against the banisters, and two grey men in overalls had the carpets up in the alcove next to the reception desk, and were doing something indeterminate with the floor. The doors to the ballroom were open, and a heavy smell of paint was seeping out towards us. We peered in briefly through the doors. What furniture there still was in the room was shrouded in the off-white of more ancient bed linen, and there was a dusty haze about the place, with a tang of old sandpaper and plaster dust. A discarded *Daily Mirror* lay on the sheets covering the nearest table.

"Christopher Lee's got the decorators in," said Lucy with a smile as we turned towards the lift.

In the middle of the night we were awakened by a loud clatter. It seemed to come from somewhere at the foot of the bed. Too tired to move or turn the light on, we both smiled in our half-sleep, thinking of my jokes about the poltergeist. The next morning we discovered that Lucy's small square suitcase had up-ended itself in the night. A collection of plastic bottles had rolled out onto the floor. I recognised them at once. Yesterday, they had been stacked in a pristine little row on the marble shelf in the bathroom: shower gel, shampoo, moisturiser, the usual upmarket freebies. Lucy had a weakness for such things. It wasn't uncommon for me to revisit the bathroom on checking out of a hotel room somewhere and find that she'd packed up the lot when I wasn't looking. Nine times out of ten she wouldn't even leave the soap behind. Our bathroom at home had so many of the things that it looked like a beautician's bazaar.

"I see you've been at the toiletries again," I smiled. "I reckon the poltergeist wants 'em back."

She was indignant. "We paid for them. Why shouldn't we take them?"

We had this conversation every time we went away. I agree that there'd be logic in taking half-used bottles away with us – the hotel staff would only replace them with unopened bottles, after all, and it would be a pity for those lovely little luxuries to go to waste – but we're not talking just the half-used bottles here. We generally ended up with *all* the bottles. Once, before we went away, I suggested that we should pack a selection of products scavenged from other hotels, and replace all the bottles in our new hotel room with the ones we'd brought, just to confuse the hotel staff. Apparently that was silly, so we just helped ourselves to the lot.

Breakfast was a bit of a disaster that morning. Quite how half the contents of the little silver teapot ended up down my right sleeve I'm not entirely sure; I swear I was pouring straight, and paying close attention to where the tea was flowing. Still, at least I didn't up-end an entire bowl full of banana flakes and muesli in the short journey from the buffet bar to our table. It was Lucy's privilege to do that. The waiter tutted at us as he mopped up the spillages with a pristine white napkin, and we decided it was wise to beat a hasty retreat.

"I'm sure I packed all these before we went down for breakfast," Lucy said, looking at the disordered array of clothes on the bed. "Hey, have you put the toiletries back?"

I hadn't; but somebody had. They had come out of her case and were back in a neat little row on the bathroom shelf. Lucy made a defiant noise through her nose and packed them again. Before too long we were on our way. A gentle stroll to the railway station, a short wait on a chilly concourse, and soon we were home, with our stash of ill-gotten toiletries safely stowed away on the groaning rack beneath the bathroom sink. At least, that's what I supposed. The next morning, they were all over the floor, and guess who had to pick them up.

"Right," I said determinedly. "This has gone too far." I reached into the morass for the thin green bottle of shower gel that we had recovered from the hotel, and slammed on the hot water.

I think I lost count of the number of broken light bulbs, crumpled shirts, and radios switched on in the middle of the night that plagued me in the next couple of weeks. Once, I even came down to breakfast to find the washing machine in the final throes of a high-speed spin cycle. It was empty, and neither of us would admit to setting it going. I was sure that those wretched toiletry bottles were to blame, so I was determined to make sure we got our money's worth out of them. I don't think I've ever showered as much as I did in those two weeks. I'd certainly never moisturised before. Lucy was starting to think I was beginning a mid-life crisis by the time I finally consigned the moisturiser bottle to the recycling bin, along with the bottles of shampoo and shower gel that I'd finished off nearly a week earlier. That was it; our supply was finished.

I was barely awake when the commotion next morning intruded into my consciousness. I have half a memory of seeing a dustbin man being chased down the road by a levitating wheelie bin, its lid snapping open and shut like the fangs of a demented crocodile. Quite how he managed to wrestle the contents into the back of his wagon, I'm not entirely sure; but he drove away down the street in some alarm, doors banging open as if a hurricane had struck. That was the last we saw of our poltergeist. From that morning onwards, our bathroom remained blissfully quiet.

We revisited that hotel once, a few months later. The renovations had finished, the ballroom was shiny and new, and the carpets were pristine. There was no sign of the hunchbacked manservant; instead, a tall Afro-Caribbean man with a tail-coat and an enormous smile took our cases and an Irish lady of middle years came to turn down our bed linen. We slept peacefully that night; and when we left the next morning, a neat little row of luxury toiletries stood to attention on the bathroom shelf, untouched by human hands.

I think we've learnt our lesson now.

A.J. Humphrey

A.J. Humphrey lives in York and works as a research scientist. His poetry has won several prizes and he has had short stories published in various small presses. His favourite colour is Indigo and he loves twilight, fairy tales, malt whisky, folk music and Dragons. His website is www.geocities.com/andyhumphrey1971.

It's a Wonderful Life

"I can't stand it any more. I'm going to jump off the nearest bridge." Helen's outburst got the response she'd half expected – nothing.

She looked round the room. The table bore the remnants of their meal; red, gold and green garlands criss crossed the walls. Dozens of cards covered the mantelpiece, but despite all the glitter, it didn't feel Christmassy to her. Even the wonderful tree, festooned with tinsel and dozens of twinkling white lights didn't lift her spirits. All Christmas meant to her was extra work.

As she cleared the table, her brother Bob looked up from the TV. "If you're going to the kitchen, make us a coffee, will you, sis?"

"I'd rather have tea," said his wife, Patty, "and the kids could do with some more lemonade."

"I wouldn't say no to a sherry," added Helen's mother.

Safe in the refuge of the kitchen, Helen felt like crying. It was the same every year. Her brother's family descended on them like a flock of hungry vultures, eating everything in sight, but never lifting a finger to help with the chores.

It wouldn't have been so bad if they'd got her a decent present. She'd spent ages finding Patty a paperweight to add to her collection, and a silver tie pin for her brother. The children had proved even more difficult. After hours of thought, she ended up giving them tokens so they could choose their own gifts; it was so hard to know what to give teenagers these days.

All she got in return was a pair of oven gloves, and that was from all four of them.

It wasn't that the gloves weren't useful; they were,

but she longed for something more personal. Even a box of chocolates or some bath salts would have been nice, or better still, some decent perfume.

The thought made her smile. What did she need perfume for? She was forty five. Caring for her mother, and holding down a job, left her very little time for a social life, and as for romance – she'd given up any idea of that a long time ago. It was sixteen years since she'd been on a date.

As she squirted washing up liquid into the bowl, she knew what Cinderella must have felt like – slaving away from morning to night whilst everyone else went to the ball and had fun. Unfortunately, there was one big difference – Helen didn't have a fairy godmother to wave a magic wand.

As she took the drinks through to the living room, her mother gave her a rare smile. "Why don't you sit down for a minute? There's a Wallace and Gromit film on next. You like those."

"Thanks," she said, "but I haven't finished the washing up."

"Can't it wait?" asked Bob. "You've been running about like a headless chicken all day. You're giving me a headache."

Kind of you to notice, Helen thought crossly. He'd hardly moved from his chair since he arrived. And as for his children, the less said about them the better. Kylie and Harry had spent hours squabbling about whose present had cost the most money. After that, they'd hardly spoken a word, they were so wrapped up in their computer games. She hadn't seen them smile, not once. And as for saying please or thank you…. Things had certainly changed since she was a teenager.

"I'd rather get it done," she said wearily. "It'll only

get worse if I leave it."

"Isn't it time you got a dishwasher?" Patty whispered to her mother in law.

"What do we need a dishwasher for?" Mrs Cartwright replied with a chuckle. "We've got Helen."

Everybody fell about laughing, but it wasn't funny to Helen, not anymore.

Christmas should be a happy time, a time for love and laughter, a time for sharing, but her mother, who was nowhere near as frail as she made out, never lifted a finger. What made the situation even worse, was that for the past six years her brother's family had come to stay. They landed on the 23rd and stayed for at least a week, sometimes two.

They treated the house like a hotel, never bothering to make their beds or pick up the towels in the bathroom, and it wasn't just at Christmas. They came in the summer too. There was never a return invitation.

Helen wondered what they would do if she really did jump off a bridge. At least then, somebody else would have to do the washing.

Filled with an uncharacteristic rush of anger, she put on her coat and shoes, and ran from the house, but the moment she'd closed the front door, the cool breeze cleared her head, calming her down again.

She laughed. What on earth had she been thinking? The nearest bridge was only twenty feet high. If she jumped off that, all she'd get would be a soaking, and a sprained ankle. Besides, she didn't want to kill herself, all she wanted was some appreciation and the occasional kind word. It wasn't much to ask, was it?

With no better idea what to do, she decided to walk down to the river anyway. Watching the lights dance on the water always cheered her up.

As she turned the corner to approach the bridge, her heart missed a beat. A man was clambering up on to the wall. Surely he wasn't thinking of jumping? He could hurt himself.

She started to run. "Hey! Stop that. What are you doing?" she shouted.

To her surprise he climbed back down and smiled at her. "I'm waiting for you, of course," he said.

She didn't know what to say. There was something about the man that seemed very familiar. Then it came to her. He looked just like the angel in her favourite film.

"I don't mean to be rude, it being Christmas and all, but please, don't tell me your name's Clarence and you're an angel trying to earn his wings. I've seen It's A Wonderful Life at least a dozen times."

The man looked hurt. "My name's Graham, and I've already got my wings. See?" He did a twirl.

Helen blinked. Was there something there? No, there couldn't be, it must be a trick of the light. She shook her head to clear it. It was her own fault for having that second glass of wine with her meal. The man was obviously mad, or drunk, or possibly both. She decided to humour him. "So, Graham," she said, more calmly than she felt. "You're an angel."

"Probationary angel," he corrected her.

"Sorry, a probationary angel. But this isn't a remake of the film, It's a Wonderful Life?"

Graham shrugged. "Well yes, and no," he shuffled his feet. "To be honest, Helen, I was at a bit of a loose end. Christmas in heaven can be just a tiny bit dull, especially when you've seen it all before. I popped down to see if anybody needed my help, and I found you."

Helen decided to play along, at least until the man had left the bridge. "You mean you want to show me how

51

different things would be if I wasn't around?"

"Something like that," he admitted.

"Well you'd be wasting your time. I haven't had a wonderful life, and I'm not Jimmy Stewart. I've never saved anyone from drowning, and I know nothing about building societies. If I were you, I'd find somebody else." She took a few steps closer. "Come on, let's take a walk down the High Street and see who we can find."

But Graham didn't move. "So you're saying you're happy with the way things are?" he asked gently.

It was too much. Helen burst into tears.

"Thought not." He reached out to take her hand. "Why don't you give it a go? Come with me. I mean, what have you got to lose?"

She hesitated. The whole thing was getting rather spooky. How did he know her name? Had he really been waiting for her? Her mind whirled with all the unanswered questions. She thought about going home to the washing up and her ungrateful family, but there was something about Graham that was hard to resist. Besides, he was right. She had nothing to lose.

Wearily she gave him her hand, and shut her eyes. When she opened them again, she was shocked to find herself standing in a cemetery. "What are we doing here?" she asked nervously.

Graham pointed to one of the graves.

Helen gasped. The name on the gravestone was her mother's. According to the dates, she'd died the previous year on Christmas Day. "That can't be right," Helen said. "I've just left her."

Graham shook his head. "You don't understand," he said. "This isn't about how things are, this is what things WOULD have been like if you hadn't been there. Your mother had a fall, and because she lived alone, by the time she was found, it was too late."

"But what about my brother and his wife? They always come to stay at Christmas. Where were they?"

"They didn't visit from one year to the next. Why would they? You weren't there to do all the work."

Helen stared at the grave, expecting to feel moved, but she didn't. Most of her mother's health problems were either imagined or vastly exaggerated. Even so, she'd been happy to make the sacrifice – that was what good daughters did, looked after their widowed mothers. What upset her were the constant complaints, and the verbal abuse.

"So how do you feel?" asked Graham. "Without you, your mother wouldn't be alive today."

"I'm not sure," Helen admitted. "She's eighty two. It's not as though she was young."

Graham sighed. "Obviously you need more convincing. I know. I'll take you to your brother's. That's bound to make you see the difference you've made to others' lives." He held out his hand. "Are you ready?"

Helen nodded. It wasn't as though she had anything better to do. When she opened her eyes she was standing in a living room. Something seemed vaguely familiar, but she wasn't sure what it was.

She shivered. The room wasn't very warm, or very inviting. A few cards sat on the mantelpiece and a small plastic tree perched in one corner, but apart from those, it would have been hard to tell it was Christmas.

Her sister-in-law was stretched on the sofa watching TV. She was on her own.

"Patty looks fed up," Helen whispered.

"There's no need to whisper," Graham said, "She can't hear us. She's fed up because they couldn't afford a proper Christmas."

"Why not?" asked Helen. "Bob's got a great job. He

earns a small fortune."

"Things are different in this life," Graham reminded her. "Do you remember lending him your car, so he could get to that interview in Southampton?"

Helen nodded. "You mean when his car broke down and he couldn't afford to get it fixed? He was having a really rough time then."

"That's right, but because you weren't there to help him, he had to take the train. Unfortunately it was delayed. He missed his connection and by the time he got to the interview, it was too late." Graham sighed and shook his head sadly. "That was the last straw. He gave up trying after that."

Helen gasped. "Now I know why this room looks so familiar. It's the flat they rented when they were first married." She looked round, taking in the tired sofa and the faded wallpaper. "What happened to their lovely home and all their wonderful things?"

"They never got them. Bob goes to the pub most evenings, and Patty. Well you can see what she does."

"Where's my brother now?"

"Upstairs. He had too much to drink at lunch time. He's sleeping it off."

"And the children?"

"In their bedroom, squabbling." He turned to Helen and smiled. "See what a difference it's made, you not being here?"

She nodded. The room wasn't uncomfortable, but it was small, and the carpet was old and very worn. It was a huge contrast to the four bedroom detached house the family lived in now. Patty looked so miserable sitting there on her own, but however hard Helen tried, she couldn't feel much sympathy for her.

"So what do you think? Are you ready to go home

now, or do I need to show you something else?" Graham asked.

Helen was about to say she was ready to leave, when she had a thought. "Graham, can you take me anywhere, any time?"

"Within limits," he replied. "Yes, I suppose I can."

"Then I'd like to see what Keith Barnes has done with his life."

Graham smiled. "Was he a boyfriend?"

Helen laughed. "Almost the only one I ever had. He wanted us to get married and move to Scotland. He'd just been offered a job there, close to his old family home. I wanted to say yes, but Mum had one of her funny turns." She frowned. It wasn't until several later that she'd discovered that her mother's funny turns were just an act. "I'd feel more content with my lot if I knew that Keith was happy."

"Where can we find him?" Graham asked. "My guess is you didn't keep in touch."

She shook her head. "No, we didn't. After a while, there wasn't any point. I could never have left Mum." She thought for a moment. "We could try his mother's house. It's Christmas after all, he might be there. I remember the address – Kiln Lodge, Manor Road, Inverness."

The next time she opened her eyes, she was in a warm and cosy room where a log fire blazed in the hearth and garlands and holly wreaths covered the walls. She gasped when she spotted Keith, the man she'd once loved.

Despite the years, she recognised him at once. He was sitting at a table with four adults and five children, playing some kind of board game. The room was full of laughter and chattering voices, and the heady scent of pine needles.

Helen walked over to the table "You're sure they

55

can't see us?" she checked.

"Can't see or hear us," Graham confirmed.

She reached out, but Graham stopped her.

"There's no point. He won't feel anything."

But Helen wasn't listening. She put her hand on Keith's arm, smiling as the familiar smell of his aftershave transported her to happier times. He had less hair, most of which was grey, but he still had that same warm smile. She would have recognised him anywhere.

Her heart filled up with love. "Is he happy?" she asked. "He looks happy."

"Most of the time," replied Graham. "When his mother died, he bought his brother's share of the house, so he's got a wonderful home. And he's very happy in his work. People come from miles around to see him."

"He's still a vet?"

Graham nodded. "Best in the county," he said.

Helen swallowed hard before asking her next question. It had been niggling away at her ever since they'd arrived in Scotland. "Did he, is he.."

"You want to know if he ever married?"

She nodded.

"No, he never did."

"Then all these children, all these happy people? Who are they? Are they his family?"

"Yes." Graham pointed. "Those two over there, that's his brother Ian and his wife Dora. Opposite are his sister Lizzie and her partner James. The little ones are Keith's nephews and nieces."

She drank in every detail of the perfect Christmas scene. It was a memory she wanted to hold in her heart for ever.

"It's time to go home," Graham said at last.

Wiping away a tear, Helen took his hand. When she

opened her eyes again, she was back in Exeter, standing on the bridge over the river Exe, but this time she was alone. The strange little man was nowhere to be seen.

What was all that about, she wondered? Had she fallen asleep? If so, it was the strangest dream she'd ever had.

For ten minutes she stayed there, watching the lights dance on the water. Obviously she must have imagined the whole thing, but what if some of it was true?

What if Keith hadn't married because he'd never stopped loving her? What if he was thinking of her right now, the way she was thinking of him?

She knew she would never rest until she found out the answer to that question. The trains were running over the Christmas holiday. All she had to do was go up Scotland and see for herself; she could do with a break. Besides, her brother and his family were staying until January 3rd, it wouldn't hurt them to look after her mother for a while.

Her decision made, she turned to walk back to the house, her head held high.

Graham watched from his hiding place. Once Helen had turned the corner and disappeared from view, he shrugged and raised his eyes to heaven.

"Oh dear," he said. "It's not the result I expected, but it will have to do," then with just the tiniest flash and whisper of wings, he was gone.

Linda Lewis

Linda Lewis (a.k.a. Catherine Howard) is a full-time writer of fiction and non-fiction. She has so many ideas she hardly knows what to do with them. Her short stories are published in UK magazines such as *Take a Break*, as well as in Australia and Scandinavia. She has an agent (Broo Doherty) who is seeking a publisher for her first novel.

Web site – www.lindatorbay.co.uk and www.writespace.co.uk.

Tricks of Firelight

Snow, and severe frost, with temperatures well below freezing: the winter of war was endless, but the three of us huddled in that abandoned hut made a half-hearted attempt to get ready for Christmas.

Antek, Adam and I… The villagers called us 'boys from the forest'. Kind of Robin Hood, without Friar Tuck. There was no Maid Marian either, and certainly no bows and arrows. We fought with pistols and home-made grenades. None of our families knew where we were. They could only guess that we had gone underground, a kind of unofficial part of Poland's secret army.

"Look, the first star's come out." Antek had been clearing a small breathe-hole in the frost that iced up the only window pane.

"The Watch Night star," he said and scattered the traditional handful of straw over the log that we used as a table – we had no white cloth to put on top.

"Shepherds run to Bethlehem through the snow…" Antek tried to cheer us up with one of our beautiful Polish carols. I joined in, but Adam shook his head.

"It's not safe!" he warned. "Those patrols are still out there. The slightest sound carries…"

"Adam's right, it isn't safe," I told Antek. He stopped singing, too. "I suppose you're right," he agreed, " and yet, the night's so clear and frosty you can almost hear the stars sing." He pulled on a tattered sheepskin coat and went outside.

He didn't stay long. When he came in, stamping snow off his boots, we asked, "Well, did you hear the stars sing?"

"It was a hungry song," Antek said, ruefully. "But I heard something else. Listen. Voices certainly carry."

The tune was so, so familiar and so were the words. *Stille Nacht, heilige Nacht...* Silent night, holy night...

"*They're* allowed to sing," Adam said bitterly.

"And they're allowed feast and get drunk on stuff they've pinched from the villagers," I said. "I used to love that carol," I added. "Not now. Not after what they've done to Poland. Not after last week's murders."

The others nodded, remembering. Last week some men from our unit had raided an enemy truck. We captured their stores and set fire to the vehicle. In return the invaders attacked a whole string of villages. Men and women were lined up against a wall. Most were shot. The others were marched off to forced labour. Old people and a few traumatised children were left in burnt-out homes. Christmas dreams had turned to nightmares.

"We picked off one or two of them after that, though," Adam said. "You saved my life, you two."

"We wanted you to enjoy our Christmas goose," Antek chuckled. "Look." A smile creased his face. He reached into a sack and pulled out a greasy-looking package.

The smell of goose pate was almost too much for us to bear.

Antek laughed at the look on our faces. "There's more," he said. And so there was: hard-boiled eggs in their shells and a loaf of freshly baked bread.

"Wow!"

"Here's my contribution, boys. " I opened vodka distilled from rowanberries, a gift from a peasant woman before the attacks.

"Good health, *na zdrowie*!" We toasted each other. None of us talked about other, happier Christmasses, or about our families. We all had scars we trailed like a bird an injured wing. When Adam joked about girls I wanted to smash his face in. I'd seen my girl friend shot. I'd joined the partisans after that.

"Someone's coming!" Adam warned suddenly. We stopped talking, straining to hear.

Snowdrifts covered the countryside for miles. We'd heard wolves earlier. Now, though, the sound that reached us was nothing more sinister than a gentle knocking. Someone coughed, but stifled the noise at once.

"Shall I look outside?" I wondered.

"And invite whoever's there to our Christmas Eve supper?" Adam scoffed.

"Whoever it is, it's not the enemy," Antek pointed out. "They don't come knocking gently at the door."

"Too right…"

The soft knock came again, hesitant, afraid.

We looked at one another. We were none of us older than eighteen, but we'd learnt the feel of fear as we hid in the forests, as we'd waited in ambush for soldiers with machine guns, as we'd run and dodged and killed.

"Who's there?" Adam called.

"Help us, please." The voice was faint and hopeless. "Please open the door."

"Who are you?" Adam insisted.

"A carpenter, please sir. My wife is with me." The accent was foreign and the Polish words were carefully phrased.

Adam opened the door wide enough for us to glimpse two pale, exhausted faces.   "You're…!"

"Yes, we are Hebrews. Help us, please."

"We can't help you. It's too dangerous." Adam's voice was harsh. He shut the door. He turned to face us. He was shaking. "If the patrols come and find them here – we're dead. They'll kill us on the spot – or hang us in the market square, a public example. Maybe burn what's left of the village, as well."

He was right, of course. We'd all seen bodies dangling on the rope, tried not to read the notice round their twisted necks: *these criminals disobeyed the orders of the Master Race*.

Oh, yes, we knew. But just the same Antek picked up his straw mattress and feather quilt.

"Where are you going with those?" Adam and I wondered.

"The barn, of course, where we camped before we found this hut."

"Antek, no, it's too dangerous. You heard how close the soldiers are. A patrol could arrive any minute – and they won't be serenading us with *Stille Nacht*," we objected.

Antek just nodded. He pushed past us and opened the door. I snatched up sacking and a heavy coat one of the peasant women had handed in before the massacre. I followed Antek outside.

The cold took my breath away. So did the stars. I can't remember ever having seen them so bright.

"They'll bring the patrols," I thought uneasily.

It wasn't far to the barn, but the woman could no longer walk. Her husband half carried her along.

Antek put his shoulder to the broken door. It creaked open. He shone his torch around the barn. Snow had got in through the holes in the roof and drifted through broken spars of wood. I shivered.

The man noticed. "It's better here than outside in the snow," he said.

"But it's still not the best place for your wife." Antek glanced at the woman and looked away, embarrassed. "You'll need water," he said.

"There's plenty of wood," the man said. "I'll light a

fire and melt some snow."

The woman moaned. Her lips were white. She'd bitten them so much that they were bleeding.

Antek spread his bedding on the ground. I held out the coat. It smelt of sweat and dung. The woman took it. We helped them get a fire going in stones we set in the middle of the floor.

"We escaped from the execution pits," the man told us. His voice shook. "They counted us first, took a census of the whole community. Then they turned their guns on us. We managed to hide, but we heard everything…"

His wife laid a warning hand on his arm.

"Thank you for helping us," she said in Polish. Her eyes glittered in her pale face. I realised she wasn't any older than us, if as old. Only her swollen shape and hunger and pain made her seem older. I think we felt very young as we retraced our footsteps to the hut.

We shared straw from our bedding with Antek, finished the bread and the goose pate and lay down. I must have slept, because when I was next aware of anything it was the empty place beside me. I sat up. It was close on midnight.

There was no sign of Antek. I guessed where he'd gone and I decided to follow him.

The stars were brighter than ever. I didn't need my torch to find the barn. It glowed amidst starlight and snow. Light spilt out of every hole and chink.

Did they want to bring the patrols? But I was drawn to the light like a child to a candle-lit Christmas tree.

And then, I thought it was all a dream.

There were all there: the two parents bent proudly over their new-born child. And Antek, his bony face soft and boyish.

Shepherds must have been too, no doubt attracted by

the light as they made their way to a muffled midnight Mass among old men and women and a few desolate children. A sheepskin lay across the make-shift cradle.

And the three kings? I don't know, but as I stared around the barn it seemed as though kings had left treasures. Perhaps it was just the effect of that goose pate on my unaccustomed, starved stomach. Or perhaps it was just wishful thinking that winter in the midst of war – but I was sure I caught a glimpse of gold, and a flash of gems. My senses were filled with fragrance. Doves fluttered among the rafters. The mother held her baby close, lifted her head and smiled.

I think I had not seen such a beautiful face.

Her husband bent and put more wood on the fire.

Flames licked the wood and lit the barn. Now I could see the holes in the roof and the cracks in the walls. Of course it was all a trick of firelight. The wood gave off that sweet smell, the flames flickered like gold, and the fluttering doves were simply drifting ash and smoke.

Then the man said, phrasing foreign, Polish words with difficulty, "Tomorrow the villagers will drive us away. Or patrols kill us and the child."

There was a shiver of fear now. The firelight dimmed. The wood was nearly used up. Only the mother still smiled, bent over her child.

I touched Antek's arm. "Let's go," I told him. "We can't do anything more for them."

"Yes, we'll go," Antek agreed.

Almost as though she'd understood, the girl looked up and said something in her own language.

"She said 'peace'," her husband translated.

"And to you and the child," Antek replied.

"Good luck," I said, turning away. Antek allowed me to hurry him back to our hut.

I suppose we slept. I dreamt of war, of marching soldiers, machine gun fire and death in the snow. I seemed to hear Antek's voice, saying, "Herod's soldiers." When I awoke yellow daylight streaked the snow around the frost-covered window of the hut.

There was no breakfast. We smoked, on the alert for patrols. Perhaps they would come that day, perhaps the next.

"What happened to those two refugees and their baby?" Adam asked.

We went out to have a look. The barn was empty. There was no sign of a baby, no firelight, no glimmer of gold, nor doves of peace. Fresh snow had fallen, blanketing, obliterating... There were no footprints to be seen except the ones we made in the soft, shining snow.

We went back to the hut and sat smoking, watching the snow. It fell thickly, covering forests and fields and ruins where homes had been. Winter held the world in its grip, an endless winter of war.

Jenny Robertson

Jenny Robertson has lived and traveled in Russia, Poland and Ukraine. A published writer of fiction and non-fiction as well as four collections of her own poems, she is now concentrating on children's fiction with Polish themes. She is delighted to be included in this Advent Anthology.

Midge and the Pony

"C'mon, Midge, if you can't keep up then you can't be in our team," and Kenny Black gave Midge a mighty shove that knocked him face down on to the grass, before he ran off to join his team mates.

Midge got to his feet and watched the other boys as they ran about kicking and dribbling the ball. It was the same every time he went out with his friends; no matter what they played at, he was too small and always last at everything. He sighed and rubbed his face with his grubby hands, he was going home – he didn't even like football.

As Midge started to walk away, he looked back; not one of the boys even noticed him going. He knew why they called him Midge; they probably thought he was a wee nuisance, like the annoying tiny midges that flew around them and left their arms and legs itchy and red on windless days.

The field where they played was really a big grassy waste ground that the village hadn't found any other use for. To get home, Midge had to walk up past a stream and round by the farmer's fields. He stopped as he always did at the field nearest to home. The two horses, both a chestnut brown colour, were grazing as usual. Midge stared at them longingly; that was what he really liked – horses. He had asked over and over if he could learn to ride, but his mum's answer was always the same.

"You know we can't afford something like riding lessons, Mark, since your dad died and anyway you're a bit small yet for even a pony you know." And she always finished with, "Wait till you're older and you might get a pony ride at the beach."

As Midge watched the smaller of the horses nuzzle

the other one before they cantered off across the field, he longed to be on the back of one, riding off like the boy in a film he had seen on television. He was nine already and somehow he thought he was never going to get much taller.

The next day at school, Miss Kerr his favourite teacher, made an announcement. "Boys and girls, listen please. We're hoping to go on a school trip next month and we need you to ask your parents for their permission and some of the cost. I have a letter for you to take home and a form you must return by next Friday."

Midge listened half-heartedly; it would probably be another boring visit to a museum or a half-ruined castle or something. He yawned and stared out the window that overlooked the hills and wished he was up there with the horses. Then his ears pricked up as Miss Kerr's voice got through to him. What had she just said?

"What did she say," Midge hissed to Kenny who was sitting beside him. "Where are we going?"

"You should have listened, cloth ears," Kenny hissed back. "Anyway, it wouldn't be any use for you, you would just fall off."

"Fall off what?" Midge was nearly jumping up and down with frustration and had turned to ask Gemma on his other side, when he felt a hand on his shoulder.

"Is something wrong, Mark?" Miss Kerr was standing at his side, arms crossed and eyebrows raised like she always did when she asked a question.

"I...I didn't hear where we're going Miss," Midge mumbled. He hated annoying Miss Kerr.

"We're going to a big Country Centre where we'll be able to try some pony riding and mucking out stables. If you all get on with your work for the rest of the day that is, and if your parents let you go."

Ponies? Midge couldn't believe it. He was in such a daze that twice Miss Kerr had to ask if he was feeling all right. He did feel a bit sick, but he knew it was probably excitement at the thought of the day out, like when his aunt and uncle were taking him to the pantomime last Christmas.

Midge couldn't wait to tell his mum and didn't even bother to take his jacket off before he gave her the letter.

"I can go, can't I Mum, please?" He couldn't bear it if she said no. He watched all the expressions on his mum's face and wondered why she didn't say anything. Surely he could go?

At last she looked at him and sighed as if she didn't know what to say.

"I know this is just what you would love to do, Mark love, but..." he saw her bite her lip. "It's the cost, dear, it's just a bit too much for me, even though the school is paying some of it...my wee job only just pays for all the extras we need..."

Midge heard her voice trail off and tried to keep the tears from showing in his eyes. He knew they didn't have as much money as some of his friends, but it had never seemed to matter so much until now. When they sat down to eat, he found he wasn't very hungry and instead of putting the television on to watch *The Simpsons*, he went up to his room to read his old copy of *Black Beauty*. His mum was quiet too and left him alone until bedtime when she came to say goodnight.

"I'm really sorry, Mark love. I know how much this means to you, but I just can't see a way to let you go. There might be another chance when you're older."

It was hearing the words, "when you're older" that made him really angry.

"There won't ever be another chance... and I'm old

enough now!" And he turned his face to the wall so he wouldn't have to see how disappointed his mum felt.

The next few days at school, Midge could hardly stand the way his friends all kept talking about the day out. When they started handing in their signed forms, he began to get desperate.

"So, where's your form then, Midge? Told you it was no use for a squirt like you," Kenny taunted.

"That's what you say, Kenny Black-heart," Midge stared up at him, determined not to admit anything to the class bully. "I just keep forgetting to bring it in."

Midge knew Kenny liked to act the bully, but he'd never actually hit anyone, apart from giving one or two smaller boys a push now and then. He just teased and taunted Midge and a few others all the time and Midge had found out the best thing to do was to answer him back and not show any fear.

But the days were going by quickly and Midge knew Miss Kerr was going to ask for all the final forms any day now. How was he going to be able to go? He still hadn't quite given up hope, but his mum hadn't said any more about the trip.

On the Wednesday after school, Midge was vaguely listening to his mum talking about the lady two doors away who was going on holiday. Then he heard the words "needing someone to look after her two rabbits..." And Midge suddenly had an idea. He loved all animals and knew a lot about rabbits from his big picture books.

"Do you think she would pay someone to look after them, mum?" He knew from her smile that she sussed him at once.

"Well, you could always ask. But what about your homework? Looking after rabbits is a lot of responsibil-ity."

69

"I could do it, I could... and you would be here so she'd know I'd look after them properly."

As soon as his mum began to smile, Midge knew he'd at least be able to ask Mrs McDonald. He quickly finished his meal, washed his hands, combed his mop of unruly brown hair and went to see her.

Half an hour later, Midge dashed in to the house and threw his arms around his mum's neck.

"I can do it, and Mrs McDonald is going to pay me something for every day...but she needs you to say you'll make sure I do it right. You will won't you, mum? And maybe I'll be able to go on the school trip?"

Midge was fidgeting about waiting for her reply and she told him to sit down for a minute.

"Let's talk about it, love. How much did Mrs McDonald say she would pay you?"

"Fifty pence each day. And that's seven days..." Midge tried to work it out. "So that's ... £3.50 for a whole week."

"And she's away for two weeks," his mum said. "So that would be £7." His mum was thinking. "I know the pony riding means more than anything else to you, Mark. I've been putting away a small amount each week for things like your birthday and Christmas. Maybe you could have part of your birthday early?"

Midge held his breath while his mum worked it out.

"I could make up the other £5 you need for the trip, and if you earn any extra you can use that for spending money."

Midge threw himself into her arms and held her tight. Sometimes he felt like crying at the silliest times, like when he was so happy he couldn't say a word.

Next morning at school, Midge walked proudly out to the front to hand in his form and stuck out his tongue at

Kenny on the way back to his seat. He'd soon see who could stay on a pony.

The time went even more quickly for Midge since he'd started looking after the rabbits, and even when Mrs McDonald came back from holiday, she let him carry on helping.

"I only keep them for my grandchildren's sake when they come to stay and I'm really glad of some help with them now," she told Midge.

At last, the day of the trip arrived and Midge just hoped he would manage to keep his breakfast down on the bus journey, he was that excited.

When the bus drove into the Country Centre, Midge saw it was huge, with walks through woods, and gardens and play areas, but he was interested in only one thing. The bus finally stopped and they all jumped down. They were here.

Then Midge could see them. Just a few yards away were the two rows of stables. When they all walked across, there they were; lots and lots of lovely ponies, heads reaching curiously over the half doors. He waited in an agony of impatience as Miss Kerr made sure everything was organised and ready. Then they met the staff and were told they would be feeding the ponies, grooming them and mucking out the stables first before they would start the riding lessons.

Midge happily threw himself into the job, ecstatic just to be near the ponies. This was much better fun than cleaning out Mrs McDonald's rabbit hutch. He laughed when he heard Kenny complaining non-stop about the hard work. Then after a quick wash and their picnic lunch, it was time at last.

One by one they were matched to the ponies and given a hard hat to wear, until there was only Midge left.

"You're a bit of a little one, aren't you?" The stable hand looked him up and down and Midge was suddenly anxious. What if he was too small after all?

He could see Kenny Black laughing over at him. At the same time, Kenny's large pony nudged him from behind and Kenny jumped back with a yell. He was scared of his pony!

Just then, the stable hand turned Midge round.

"We've got just the pony for you, son, he's our special favourite."

And Midge could see one of the stable hands leading a very small white pony.

"He's Sprite, our Shetland pony, and he's just waiting for a rider like you."

Midge tentatively held out his hand and let Sprite gently nuzzle it, before he stroked the pony's shaggy mane. He knew they were going to be the best of friends.

As he put on his hard hat, he heard Miss Kerr call out just to him, "Let me get a photograph of you both, Mark, you're a perfect picture."

Midge put his arm round the pony's neck and rested his head against the little Shetland. Wait till he told his mum and Mrs McDonald. It was going to be the best day of his life; ever.

Rosemary Gemmell

Rosemary Gemmell writes non-fiction articles, poetry and fiction for adults and children. Many have been published in national magazines; some have won prizes. She is now attempting full length fiction which requires more self-discipline! She enjoys market research and sharing information with other writers.

www.rosemarygemmell.com

Winter Blooms

"Don't hold with flowers in winter," Len grumbled when I told him what I'd been doing. "They aren't natural. Winter's a time for the earth to sleep. It'd be like us staying up all day and night, otherwise." He tapped his stick on the floor of the mobile library. "There should be no flowers till the first snowdrops."

I could have pointed out the winter-flowering jasmine cascading over his garden wall, but I kept my mouth shut. He'd only say they didn't count, or something along those lines.

I didn't mind. I was used to Len, since meeting him on my first day on the 'bookbus', back in the summer. I'd been looking forward to it for weeks. My new job, that was, not meeting him. Let's face it, who wouldn't prefer travelling along winding country lanes, verges frothy with cow parsley, to being stuck in a dark building all day? I'd briefly been down similar lanes before, in the backs of cars, between foster homes. But that's another story.

"What's up with your nose?" His gruff voice that day had made me jump. Looking up, I saw opaque, almost milky, eyes magnified behind dark-rimmed glasses, a grizzled face complete with grey beard, and fingers that were stained, but not with nicotine or ink. "Had a fight with a stapler?"

"It's a nose stud, as you well know, you old fool," Jack, our driver, answered for me. "Keep up with the times, can't you?"

"I'll give you bloomin' times. Here, stamp these for me, then I can get out of the way for Hilda and her romances. I take it that isn't a problem? No spikes or anything on your hands, are there?"

The elderly lady behind him, presumably Hilda, tutted and shook her head as I tried to think of a witty retort. None sprang to mind that weren't rude, and I wasn't going to risk losing this job.

"Are there any books you'd like ordering, Mr...?"

"Just stick with Len," said Len. He winked at Jack. "Hark at her. We didn't get that with the last one. Now you mention it, I'd appreciate any art books you can dig up"

He came out with a list of names I'd never heard of. I jotted them down and hoped he didn't notice me struggling with the foreign spellings.

"See how many of those you can get." It sounded like a challenge. "And none of your Monets or Constables. Their paintings have whiskers on them."

Even as I turned to Hilda's pile of Jilly Coopers, I knew that life on this round wasn't going to be boring.

Time went past and the nights drew in. I got some bits and pieces for my bedsit, and it began to feel like a real home. Or, at least, how I thought a real home should feel. I planted up bulbs and put them on a shelf in the broom cupboard, where it was dark, so they'd be ready for Christmas.

The bookbus felt like home, too, in a way. The people who came on were the equivalent of friends and relatives. Hilda Robinson was the kindly next-door neighbour, wondering if you'd like some cuttings from her garden. Len was the grouchy old bloke across the road who turned out to be a mine of information, leaning on the gate as he told you about when he fought in the war, or what all the trees in the nearby woods were, and more besides. Then there were the mums and toddlers, come for their week's supply of bedtime books.

Along the lanes, the leaves turned and fell, abandoning branches black and skeletal against heavy skies. Our regulars wore bulky coats and blew into their hands as we drew up. Those who'd gone for more adventurous authors in warmer weather now settled for old favourites, comfort-reading their way through winter.

Not Len.

"There's nothing wrong with flowers in winter," I said to him now, in response to his statement. "They make good Christmas presents." Hilda nodded her agreement. "You should be praising me for my frugal ways, instead of complaining how extravagant the younger generation are."

Big mistake. Len was already on to it.

"I never said anything of the sort. Enjoy yourself while you're young, I always say."

I thought of mentioning the new butterfly tattoo on my left shoulder, but decided against it, wondering instead how I was going to track down his latest list of books.

Speaking of books…

"I'm afraid I didn't get on with those Jilly Coopers," Hilda said as she handed hers back. "Have you any Georgette Heyer?"

Put it down to stubbornness, but I moved Hell and high water to get those titles Len wanted.

So I was disappointed when he wasn't there. Hilda wasn't around, either.

"Would you come out if you didn't have to, in this weather?" was Jack's reaction when I mentioned our absentees. "Plenty of others haven't."

I could see his point, as rain drummed on the roof. Yet part of me wasn't convinced.

It was Hilda who told us, the following week.

"I'm afraid he had a fall," she said. "This time last week, in fact. I called round because the postman left me some of his letters by mistake, and there was no answer. So I got the key from his cleaning lady who was already at one the other houses, and we spent the morning organising an ambulance to get him to hospital. You must have just missed us."

"Which hospital is he in?" I asked, reaching for a pen and notepad.

"Oh, he discharged himself," Hilda replied. "Said he was …" she whispered a swear word, relatively mild by modern standards "…if he was staying there, and if he was going to die, he'd do it in the comfort of his own home."

Len? Die? My throat tightened.

"Is he home now?"

"Yes. With the nurse visiting, and at her wits' end, because he never does as he's told…"

I was already heading for the steps.

I knew the score. Old people fell. It was a fact of life. But Len wasn't old people. Not to me, at any rate. He was Len. And the way he'd discharged himself from hospital struck a chord. It couldn't have been easy for him to defy the doctors like that, just as it hadn't been easy for me to defy everyone's preconceptions. Children with my 'troubled' background weren't expected to pass exams. But I did it, I thought to myself as I knocked on the stained glass panelled door. I showed them.

The lady who answered introduced herself as Karen, Len's care worker.

"He'll be pleased to see someone different," she told me. "Though I warn you, he might not show it."

I soon saw what she meant.

In an armchair by the tiled fireplace sat a man who looked like Len yet somehow wasn't. The television was on. Its volume had been turned right down but on the screen I could see some sort of documentary, with a shimmering blue sea and terracotta rooftops.

"You've got a visitor, Len." Karen raised her voice as if he was half deaf. "The lady from the library. She's brought you some books."

Slowly, he turned his gaze in our direction.

"You don't have to shout," he snapped. "I'm not stupid."

But his hands shook, and he didn't make any move to pick up the books I'd just put down on a small table next to his chair.

Outside the window, spiders' webs sagged under the weight of giant raindrops and there were dead-heads on the hydrangeas. We may have been into December, with decorations brightening up the shops in town, but out here Christmas seemed no more than a distant dream. Some days, it hardly even seemed to get properly light. Nothing grew in lifeless fields, and fallen leaves had made the lanes slippery, meaning Jack had to ease the bus round so we didn't end up in the ditch. I was glad I'd planted those bulbs. I kept checking on them, on their shelf in the cupboard more and more, just to see them slowly come into bud.

"Are there any books to return?" I asked, as much to break the silence as anything. "I might as well take them while I'm here."

"They're in the bedroom." Karen bustled off, leaving the two of us alone.

Staying with so many different families, I'd been in some odd situations, but nothing quite like this. It felt wrong seeing him sitting there, pale, with a rug over his legs.

"It's been quiet on the van without you," I said.

"Jack's got no-one to argue with. He tried with Hilda, but she wouldn't rise to the bait."

Len grunted in reply, as if he'd used up his energy. I shuffled awkwardly and glanced round the room. It was full of life, though not in the usual way of knick-knacks and mementoes. Books had been squeezed into shelves at every conceivable angle until no gaps were left. Another table was covered with magazines and periodicals. And every wall displayed a collection of paintings all clearly created by the same hand. Some canvasses stood propped up in one corner, covered by a striped flannelette sheet.

Suddenly everything made sense. The stains on his hands, the books he requested. Even the documentary was now showing what looked like works by Picasso, with heads and arms in strange places.

"Why didn't you tell me you're an artist?"

"Because he never tells anyone, the awkward so-and-so," said Karen as she came back into the room. "He's a dark horse, our Len. Did you know he used to exhibit in London? If that was me, I'd be shouting it from the roof-tops. But him? Honestly, you just don't know, with some people."

"No, you don't," I wanted to tell her. I never knew why everyone was so surprised I wanted to be a librarian. I love books. I always have. One day you can be all goosebumps from reading a horror story, the next all weepy from a wartime romance.

The van's horn sounded outside.

I took the books from Karen. "I'd better be going. We're running late already. But I'll be back next week," I added, pointedly, to Len.

As I rushed down the path, I glanced back through the window. Was it my imagination, or did he raise his hand ever so slightly?

Whether he did or not, I reckoned the two of us had a lot in common. We were both 'different', both fed up of people telling us what to do. I wished I could help, even if only a little. And I already had an idea.

When Karen opened the door a week later, her smile turned to a gasp. "Good Lord! Here, let me give you a hand."

Len was in the armchair again, watching another documentary, about some kind of subterranean lake, with people drifting in boats in the semi-darkness.

"You took your time."

He still had a rug over his legs, but there were two sticks propped by the chair.

"It's the same time as usual, and you know it," I said.

"Hmmmph. Let's see what books you brought, seeing as you were let loose to choose."

I handed them over. This time he took them, though I suspected it cost him some effort. While he turned the pages, I sneaked a look at some of the paintings.

"These are really good," I couldn't help saying.

"They should be. I've been painting pretty much all my life."

"Do you still paint?"

"What do you think those are?" He nodded towards the stack of canvasses I'd seen before..

"Can I look?" I moved towards them.

"No! They aren't finished. They're the ones I was working on before I stupidly fell."

"There's nothing stupid about falling. Everyone does sometimes."

"You sound like one of those nurses. You'll be trying to plump my pillows next."

Perish the thought. "Sorry," I said. "I didn't mean it

like that. I know how annoying people can be, even if they mean well. Especially if they mean well," I added, half to myself.

He raised his eyebrows but didn't pursue the matter further.

"So when are you going to finish them?"

He slumped back. "I won't. I'm not so steady with a paintbrush any more."

For a second, I wanted to take one of his walking sticks and poke the floor with it, just as he had in the library van. "Not so steady? You could be blindfold and still do a brilliant job. I bought some cards by those artists who have to use their feet and so on. I bet they felt like giving up loads of times, but they didn't." Karen frowned and shook her head frantically at me, but I ignored her. "Feel free to sit here and carry on watching the box if that's what you want," I continued. "But don't blame me if you end up like the people in that boat, drifting in the dark."

In the astonished silence that followed my little speech – or outburst, depending on how you see it – the van's horn made us all jump.

There was just one more matter before I left.

"This is for you," I said, thrusting a semi-wrapped parcel at him. Well, it had to be semi-wrapped, didn't it? I wasn't going to risk my babies being squashed.

Despite the slight tremor still in his hands, Len opened it himself. It took him a minute but he managed it.

"Why, you cheeky…" Luckily the last word was drowned out by another blast from the horn.

Which brings me to today, our last round before Christmas. You can't say we didn't make an effort, though it was a nuisance when half the tinsel kept falling down every time we went round a corner. Jack had a tiny plastic Christmas tree suctioned onto the dashboard. We both even wore Santa hats.

Our regulars stamped their feet against the cold and swore it was going to snow. For some reason, murder mysteries seemed popular. Maybe it was the thought of all those relatives about to descend. Children's story books went well, too, presumably to help them settle on The Night.

When we came to Len's stop, there were so many people waiting, I couldn't abandon Jack. Besides, I wasn't sure I'd be welcome after my last performance..

Hilda went against the grain and opted for some Charles Dickens.

"I always read him at this time of year. He's so Christmassy, don't you think?"

Then came the first surprise.

"It's been wonderful to see how you've come on over the past few months," she said, placing her hand on mine. "You've positively blossomed."

Positively blushed, more like. I was speechless.

Thanks to the second surprise, though, I didn't need to reply.

"Blossomed? *Blossomed?* Talk sense, woman!"

We all turned at the sound of that unmistakable voice. Somehow, with the aid of two walking sticks and the long-suffering Karen, Len had made it onto the van.

"What were those books you got me?" I tried to keep a straight face as he thrust a finger towards me. "Because of you, I've had to come out just to get something decent."

Karen's exasperated sigh could probably be heard halfway across the village, but I didn't care. When he got her to pick out some gruesome murder mysteries, growling instructions at her while he had a sit-down, I knew for certain he was on the mend.

Then there was the third surprise... but I'll tell you about that in a minute.

Afterwards, as we drove off past Len's house – complete with hyacinths flowering vigorously in his front window – it started to snow. Within half an hour, a pristine blanket lay across fields and garlanded trees. At long last, it looked like a scene from a Christmas card.

"You won't be so pleased if we get stuck," warned Jack, but he was smiling even as he said it.

"No opening it till Christmas Day," Len had warned when he handed me the brown paper parcel. That was the third surprise. I'm afraid I didn't wait – just as he didn't wait to be thanked. I opened it as soon as I got home this evening. The painting is hanging on the wall even as I write.

If you're familiar with his work, you'll probably find it hasn't as much detail as you might expect. He's still recovering, after all. But the boldness of style and vibrant use of colours are unmistakable nonetheless. He's signed it, of course. Even given it a title.

You mean you haven't already guessed? I must admit I hadn't either, though I could have kicked myself when I saw it.

"Winter Blooms." Or, as I call it, "The Best Christmas Present I Ever Had."

Rebecca Holmes

Rebecca Holmes has short stories published in national women's magazines and occasionally remembers to work on her first novel, a contemporary family saga set in the Lake District. She lives in Leicestershire with her husband and their two daughters, plus two elderly rabbits and a juvenile cat.

On the Feast of Stephen

The removal van arrived very early in the morning. Before we were out of bed even. But we heard the thrum of the engine, felt it in our bones as it rattled about the half empty rooms. The sound of men's voices cut sharply through the frosted air and the smell of diesel crept through the ill-fitting windows. It was time to go.

I pushed back the covers on my bed and swung my feet out onto the bare floor. Carpets had been lifted the day before; it felt cold and unwelcoming, as if the house were already beginning to shrug us off. Looking back I am not sure if this made leaving easier or harder. For in this house are my roots.

I was born in the tiny room above the kitchen. It was used specially so, for below us a great wood burning stove glowed warmly against the cold winter months. For the first weeks, my Mother wanting me close, kept me there by her side where I could sleep and feed and feel the steady beating of her heart and dream that I was still in the womb. It was a time for rest, my Mother said, and a time for quiet, so that we should know each other well, without distraction from the outside world. It was a good time, she said.

But even good things can change and one day Father came home with a new birch-wood crib which he set by her side.

"For new beginnings." He said placing me in it and instantly broadened my horizons from the shadowy depths of my parents' bed to a new soft snowy world of lace and duck feather. On the end of my crib a glass charm, which my Father had made in his workshop, twirled prettily and caught the weak winter sun, and from this splinters of brightly coloured light wheeled about the room. In the afternoons, when the sun was low, one of these little pools of light would fall directly upon Mother's bed and she would take me up and nurse me so that I might watch the dust motes soaring in the air above.

There is no such warmth today. The stove has been let to go out and the sun is hidden behind a veil of silver grey mist which trails through the treetops and catches on the rocky outcrops that surround our house. Mother is downstairs giving directions to the removal men and Father, I suspect, is saying goodbye to his beloved workshop.

Father, whose name is Wenceslas, after our patron saint, is very sad to be leaving, even though it is because of him that we are going. Bohemia, you see, is very famous for its glass and lead crystal and Father is very good at making such beautiful things. Here though, he is one of many, but in England... a man there... he has seen some of Father's work. He wants him to go and show him his secrets. It is a great opportunity.

That is what they say.

But let me tell you about the workshop. For it is full of magic, like walking through a fairy tale or enchanted land. At least this is how it has always seemed to me: Glass is everywhere, shimmering and swaying, filling the room with light until it sparkles like sun dappled water on a mid summer's day. Chandeliers, baubles, angels with outspread wings, all float in the air and cast their spells upon the animals and trinkets that nestle below amongst soft white tissue. Sometimes the light makes them ripple with life. It is as though they stretch and crane to see what he is doing. And sometimes they speak. Sometimes a gentle movement of air wakes them. And then eyes begin to glitter and to smile. "Tell us who we are." They whisper. "Tell us."

"Krystina…"

Mother is shouting me to go down.

So now I must pull on my socks and tie up my heavy boots, for it is cold out and we have a long journey ahead of us. I must stand up and leave my room – for the last time. But before I do I take my special trinket out of my pocket and place it on the window ledge where I leave it to gather dust. I am not sure why I do this. Except I am angry. Inside I am angry and I am frightened.

I leave the room without looking back.

Downstairs I eat a hurried breakfast; yesterday's bread and some cheese. Mother scurries round packing a bag of all things necessary to our journey: more food, apples, some cake, a flask of hot milky coffee. Father sits and looks very pale and I notice that when he smiles it is quite wooden. His family have lived here for six generations he says. But now it is time to move on.

"We are lucky Krystina. We can take our dearest possessions with us to make us feel at home in our new country." He is saying this with his mouth. Yet I wonder if he knows that his eyes are saying a completely different thing.

I want to answer, to shout, no. No, we are not lucky. This is a mistake. I want to say that I am frightened. I am frightened that in leaving everything I have ever known I will begin to forget who I am. That I will be forgotten.

But my tongue is stuck fast to the roof of my mouth and Mother, who has gone outside to organise last minute things in the car, calls for us to go. It is a relief. I am glad she calls because it is too late for such conversations now. And it stops me from crying.

So. I think, we do not even wait for Christmas day.

So. I think, we are leaving our house, our friends, everything that is familiar to us. And worse – We are leaving Grandma, even though England is such a long way away and Grandma is old.

So.

Then Father takes his coat from the back of the door. He stands and looks at me and smiles his wooden smile. "Best put on our coats." He says. And turns to open the door for me to pass through. Silently I go out. Out into the cold air where my breath curls away from me like dragon smoke and the removal van waits impatiently for us to leave and the men fidget to come in and finish emptying our house. The back doors of the van stand open and a ramp runs down onto the frozen ground. Condensation drips forlornly from its sides like huge tears.

Father comes out of the house after a final look round and climbs into the car.

"Ready" Mother shouts a little too gaily and climbs into the car also. The men begin to walk down the path towards the house that is no longer ours and I turn away and climb into the back of the car. We move slowly off into the pristine snowy whiteness of early morning.

The car begins to pick up speed. And I panic. Now suddenly, there is too much to take in. Air is punched out of me. It has all been too quick. I think I am going to be sick. It seems I left the house too quickly after all. I should have walked about my room, touched the walls, the window frame, looked out at the view, lain back on my bed as a thin sliver of sun fought its way out through the mist and painted the bottom of my coverlet gold. I should not have left my trinket. And worst of all, I should have said good-bye one last time to my friends, to Grandma...

A great shudder of cold passes through me. Ahead trees lean over the road, casting blue, grey shadows. It is as though there is ice in my veins. Even tears are frozen, locked tight inside. Right now, at this very moment it is difficult to believe that I will ever feel warm again.

And then I must have fallen asleep for the next thing I remember is my Mother gently waking me.

"We are here Krystina, we are in Prague." She smiles and strokes my hair.

"Mother...I..."

"Ssh my darling," she says "for it is important that we enjoy this time. Now come."

She holds out her hand. I can feel my eyes glittering. I feel like one of Father's glass animals waking up after a long sleep and I look about me with wonder.

Prague is very beautiful.

The evening light is painting the city scarlet and the golden spires of St Vitus Cathedral are drawn about with a deep blue from the sky. Somewhere I can hear music playing and the smell of food cooking reminds me that I am hungry. Despite myself I feel the first small stirrings of looking forward.

This is to be a special time. A holiday before we leave. A time for looking and a time for seeing. Without distraction Mother says placidly. She is right. In the past our visits to Prague have been all tied up with Father trying to do business; all hurry and bustle and Father worrying that he has not sold enough of his precious glass. And Mother busy stocking up on provisions against the snowy winter months. This time though we have no worries about blocked roads or long days and nights when we are unable to leave our house even.

We take our bags out of the car and go into the hotel where we are staying.

"Petrin Hill" Father says at breakfast next morning. "We shall climb Petrin Hill and look out over the city."

"I should like to visit the castle and to walk... slowly..." Mother emphasises the last "across Charles

Bridge."

Father raises his eyebrows quizzically.

"You know there are thirty statues along that bridge. Saints and religious figures that I feel I ought to become better acquainted with..." she says.

"They are reproductions, you know that. If you wish to meet the real thing then it is the museums you need to visit." Father interrupts laughing. And then he turns to me. "And how about you little one. What would you like to do?"

I shrug my shoulders. "I don't know. Wenceslas Square perhaps. And I am sixteen." I add quietly.

"Yes." Mother watches me closely. "She is sixteen, Wenceslas. You mustn't forget that."

"Aah, so I am told." He says and leans back in his chair. "Then perhaps we must leave you to your own devices, eh?"

"No." I say. For that is the last thing I want. To be alone in a place where I know nobody.

In the end we think we shall go into the city and just look about. Father says that perhaps we should find a tourist guide and do it properly. But Mother refuses to do this and says she is not that much of a stranger to her capital city.

"And" she says "we shall leave Petrin Hill until the last." On this she is quite determined.

I run upstairs for my camera, which I left lying on the bed. When I come down again Mother and Father are already outdoors waiting for me.

It is a lovely day. The cold winter sun glistens upon the snow and Prague has never looked more pretty. On Charles Bridge we look into the Vltava and see beneath us a myriad of phantom spectres, tiny circles of rainbow colour, suspended in the early morning mist that rises from the river. I click away with my camera and hope that I have caught it just right. Next we go to Wenceslas Square and again I take pictures. It seems there are a million things I have never noticed before. Plaques and carvings, obscure house signs from the days before they were given numbers; two ornate golden suns above one door, three lilies above another, a devil, a green lobster...

The day passes in a whirl and that evening we sit at a pavement cafe drinking hot chocolate. The cafe owner has a brazier going and so we warm ourselves and stare into the flames as if to see what tomorrow will bring.

And so the days pass and all too soon we find it is the time to walk up Petrin Hill. Mother arranges for us to have an early breakfast and a packed lunch. Somehow she is strangely agitated and insists that we take blankets to sit on, even though Father says it will be too cold to hang about. I look at her questioningly but she just continues to fluster. Twice she looks in the mirror and pats her hair. I notice that she slips a lipstick in her handbag. I look at Father but not even he seems to know what she is thinking of.

"You must wrap up extra warmly." She says before we leave. And runs through a check list of scarves and gloves and hats, much like she did when I was little. Then she checks again that I have spare batteries for my camera. It is not until she is absolutely sure that everything is in order that we are we allowed to leave.

Petrin Hill is three hundred metres high and Father says it is not a hill for running up. Besides he wants to see inside St. Michael's Church and to explore the Mirror Maze and The Hunger wall. But Mother is insistent that we keep going and hurries us on.

"We could have taken the funicular to the top." He says panting after her.

Mother ignores him and marches on. Something tells me she is relieved to find the Mirror Maze is not open until next summer and that St. Michael's Church is closed to the public. "If you are hungry" she says "then we can eat at the top."

And so she continues to chide us until at last we break through the trees and come out upon the summit. I am surprised to see how many people are already there. And how many more are getting off the little train that has just arrived at the top. I watch with interest and smile as they stamp their feet with the cold. For I am warm with the exertion of walking and of course, all the extra clothes mother has made me wear.

Mother takes Father over to the observation tower and sends me to look at the timetable for return trips down the hill. "Just in case your father gets too tired." She says and pushes me off.

I walk off towards where the newly arrived group of people are standing huddled about the notice board. One of them has a hat on just like my own. It is distinctive because it has two long tassels of bright yellow wool hanging down the back. And then I notice that the girl's coat is familiar too. Am I dreaming? Is it? Zofie?

The girl turns round and smiles. "Hello Krystina." She says and holds out her hands to me. And suddenly I am surrounded by smiling faces, familiar faces, faces that I have grown up with, laughed and cried with. I look round and they are all there. Friends from school, people from our church, neighbours, villagers and best of all Grandma.

Grandma is stood amongst them. Right in the middle. Someone has hold of her by the arm, taking care she is safe.

"But how...why...?" I am overcome with emotion.

90

My friend hugs me. "Did you think we should let you go so easily?" She whispers in my ear. And in doing so begins to melt the tears that have been clustering around my heart this past six months.

And then we are all shaking hands and smiling and kissing each other on the cheek. And in the midst of all this Grandma raises a hand to speak and we grow quiet.

"We stand here today, we all stand here, on the threshold of change, none more so than my son and his family. But let me tell you that change is not always bad. Sometimes it is good and sometimes not even this, sometimes it just is and then we learn to make the best of it. Now remember this. That Prague itself stands for threshold and it is from here, this beautiful place, that they will move forward into a new life..." she falters and looks towards my Father.

And it is then that I notice he is crying. And she stops speaking and puts her arms around him and Mother puts her arms round both of them. Someone begins to sing a carol. Softly at first but gathering strength as others begin to join in. And soon we are all singing and the mood is changed as we lay out blankets and food and open flasks of steaming hot soup. And someone unfolds a camping chair and offers it to Grandma who thanks them kindly but makes Father sit in it.

And because she is fond of speeches she raises her hand again and announces

"Today is The Feast of Stephen."

Everybody claps.

How fitting" she continues "that we are all here overlooking Prague on this very special day – like the saints themselves, who must be looking down too..."

But she gets no further because everybody starts to clap again, more vigorously this time, so that she will not make Father cry again. I look about at all the smiling faces and think, of course, I should have known, this is exactly as mother planned it.

It is a wonderful day. And I take many photographs. And later, when my friend Zofie is leaving, she asks me not to forget her.

"Never." I say shocked.

"Me neither." she shakes her head.

"We will write and we will visit in the holidays." We say together.

And we both laugh and somehow amongst all the tears of farewell I feel much stronger than I have done in a long time.

And now there is only one more thing to tell you and that is of our arrival in England.

My first impression is of a grey, miserable place. The airport buildings look like an assortment of giant boxes scattered upon the ground. I think they are made of concrete. It is all very ugly. In the cafe where we sit and wait to be collected, someone, a child perhaps, has written their name in the misted windows. We smile small, thin smiles at each other and wait. Eventually a woman comes to find us. She is sorry to be late but her husband has had to go out and help a neighbour who is having trouble with their car. In this, I think relieved, it is not so very different to home.

Quickly she bundles us outside and into an old van. To us it seems like she drives at breakneck speed. But it is to beat the weather, which she tells us is closing in fast. It is not a comfortable journey. And we do not attempt much speech as the van is very noisy.

When we get out of the van we are stiff and disorientated. I try to make out our surroundings even though in the dark it is difficult to tell whether you will like a place or not.

"You are not far from the village here." The woman tells mother as we walk up the path to the front door. In the morning, she says, we will be able to see the hills from our front window. So I am hopeful.

She fumbles her way in through the front door and I hear her hand searching along the wall for the light switch. I hear a click but nothing happens. Then she mutters something under her breath and suddenly she turns and leaves us standing in the dark. "Wait there." she shouts over her shoulder as she hurries back down the path. And then we hear the sound of the van's engine starting up and driving off into the distance. We stand bereft in the cold hallway, wondering where else she imagines we might go.

It does not feel like a good start.

We are just beginning to think we have been left for good when a man's voice calls out of the gloom to us. We peer out into the darkness and see nothing. "Hello there." Father shouts uncertainly and after a while the man's voice returns.

"Just coming." he shouts.

He is still not visible but from the direction of his voice there is a soft red glow hovering about four or five feet off the ground. It is all very strange.

We hear the garden gate creak open and footsteps coming down the path. And all the while the light is coming closer.

"Soon have you." says the voice again.

I take hold of Mother's hand.

Then at that moment the clouds part and the stars come out and in front of us a man is standing holding a shovel of burning hot embers.

"For the fire" he says by way of explanation and then adds "sorry I wasn't here earlier." And he smiles.

After this everything happens at once. The woman returns with a light bulb and also her husband who holds out his hand in welcome, first to my Father and then to my Mother and then me. Another woman, round and cheery, appears with a huge saucepan of soup and homemade bread. Behind her a girl, about my age smiles shyly at me. The fire roars up the chimney.

"If I were you" says the man who brought the fire shovel after we have all eaten "I would get upstairs and nab the room above this. It's the warmest in the house."

Over the table I catch my Mother's eye and she smiles at me knowingly.

"Thank-you." I say "that is good advice."

Before I leave the room the girl, whose name is Sally, asks me if I would like to walk with her the next day. She will take me to the village and there I can meet her friends. We arrange for her to come shortly after breakfast.

That night I sleep better than I had ever imagined would be possible. And even though I dream of home it is not a sad dream.

The next morning when I wake the house is very quiet. I stretch my arms and lie for a while with my eyes closed. Without distraction I think. So that I may get to know you well. It is in this way that I feel the sun before I see it.

Now I think, now I am ready. I open my eyes.

At the bottom of my bed hangs the glass trinket. Father. He must have seen it on the window ledge and picked it up. My heart leaps. Splinters of brightly coloured light twirl about the room. One of them rests golden upon my cover and I gently move my hand through the light while above me the dust motes soar...

Annie Bates

Annie's father was an artist. She spent long hours, as a child, watching him trying to capture a certain light, a nightscape, sun rippling over water, because she cannot draw at all, it now seems entirely natural to her to try and capture the essence of life on the page in words, which she loves.

Dancing Man

The Dancing Man was performing on the pavement at the side of the road. He had the windowless wall of the social club behind him, and in front, across the road, a grassy slope which led away to a low cliff and a restless sea. Graham parked some distance away and watched him for a few moments. A driver tooted. Graham watched to see if the Dancing Man reacted to this, but wasn't surprised to see he didn't.

For his first approach, Graham decided to keep his notebook hidden. God knows if he'd get any sense out of him anyway. He'd asked the police about him and they claimed they didn't know anything. Even his sources were no use. Their silence only made Graham more curious.

"Hi," he said, standing on the pavement about twenty feet away.

The Dancing Man didn't respond. His clothes were scruffy but in direct contrast, Graham noticed, were his shoes. They looked like new, gleaming in the sunlight.

"Fancy a chat?" Graham asked amiably.

There was no reply.

"How about a coffee? I'll buy."

Graham watched him through the silence, wondering if his moves had a pattern. He stepped forwards, then backwards, arms waving in front of him. Sometimes they'd fly above his head, as if throwing confetti. Every so often there would be an extravagant twirl, but there was little grace in the movement.

"I don't even know if you can hear me, but you're not blind, are you? You can see me. You could at least stop for a moment."

The Dancing Man wasn't about to stop.

Graham took out his notebook and wrote a message.

He walked forward slowly, waited for a gap in the traffic, then stepped into the road to get in front of the Dancing Man, while staying out of arm's reach.

"Hello? Hello? Can you see me?" Graham waved his hands.

He didn't think the Dancing Man was blind, but there was no flicker of recognition. Another passing car gave them a blast on the horn.

Back on the pavement, Graham said, "I'm a newspaper reporter. I should be in court but I told my editor I had a better story. You."

The Dancing Man did a funny shuffle with his feet, like a child testing an icy pavement. For a moment Graham wondered whether it meant something, then dismissed it.

"I'll cut to the chase," he said. "You're the town's village idiot. The Dancing Man. Strutting his stuff every day by the social club. Only no-one knows anything about you. Do they? No-one knows your name, for one thing." He paused, waiting for a response he never expected. Or got. "Will you talk to me? This is your chance to tell people who you are, and why you do…this."

Tap tap tap of the Dancing Man's feet.

"Either you talk to me, and I get the facts, or you don't talk to me, and I make my own conclusions. Get things wrong. Make you look even more ridiculous."

The Dancing Man did the funny shuffle again.

Graham looked out at the sea, keeping the Dancing Man in the corner of his eye. He could feel the heat of the sun on his face, and its warmth bouncing back off the wall behind him. "I'll say this," he said. "You've picked a good spot to be insane."

The Dancing Man did his awkward twirl.

"I'm coming back tomorrow with a photographer,"

Graham said finally. "If you don't talk I'll just ask the neighbours. Neighbours love talking. They tell you all kinds of things. Occasionally things that are right."

In court later that afternoon, Graham slouched on the press bench, vaguely aware of the scruffy young lad standing in the dock. Neither of them wanted to be there.

The judge refused bail. The defendant swore at him, shouted something about wearing the same clothes, and threw a pair of socks bunched into a ball. Without blinking the judge fined him £100. The lad swore at him and the fine increased to £200. Graham yawned as two court attendants bundled the defendant from the court.

The judge looked equally bored. He looked down at the clerk. "Can we call it a day?"

Graham checked his watch. It was 3pm.

Outside in the foyer he was on the phone to his editor. "That's it for the day. Nothing 'til tomorrow now."

"Well, we're light on advertising," the editor said, "We need stories – lots of space to fill yet."

Another late finish, Graham thought wearily. He slapped the mobile shut.

At just after seven that evening he called Karen, but as before there was no answer. They'd planned dinner for six. Steak. Candles. A bottle of red wine. Graham remembered saying something like, "When was the last time?"

Karen arrived home ten minutes after him. "All work and no play, and all that," she said, which was no more of an apology than Graham gave her.

He was the only one in the office early the following morning. A school kid had died from glue sniffing. He got enough detail from the police for a story but the process didn't stop there. The deadline gave him an hour to get an interview and a picture. Graham grabbed his notebook and coat.

The kid's home was on a shabby estate he knew well. Houses lined the road like rotting teeth. He parked round the corner from the house, just in case he needed to make a dash for it. Parents sometimes didn't take too kindly to the press. But that wasn't the case this time. Now he sat in his car again, underlining sections of shorthand in his notepad. In the mobile's loudspeaker he could hear Jean, the copy-taker, clacking away on her keyboard. In the background the editor was shouting about the deadline.

Graham read one of the underlined sections. "Mrs Naysmith said, colon, quote, I know a lot of people round here don't like our Billy…make that *didn't*, Jean…a lot of people round here *didn't* like our Billy."

He looked at the school photograph the mother had given him. It had stared at him from the mantelpiece while the mother talked and chain-smoked. Photographs of dead people did that. But it was just another kid. School uniform, tie hanging to the right as if someone had hastily tried to straighten it. Big mischief-making grin. Graham's police source said he had only one nostril when they found him.

"That do it, Jean?" he asked when he'd run out of things to say.

"400 words in total," Jean said.

"File it please. I'm on my way with the photo. Tell subs it's an upright."

Graham arranged to meet a photographer at the social club. He arrived first, checked the Dancing Man was there, and waited. He watched the Dancing Man through the windscreen. It was hypnotic, but not because any of the movements were silky or graceful. Far from it. Graham sat and watched, trying to put his finger on what it was, but his reverie was broken by a tap on the window.

"What's this all about?" the photographer asked.

"Follow me," Graham said, getting out of the car.

A light drizzle began to fall. Graham stood closer to the Dancing Man but there was still no flicker of recognition. No obvious change in the dance. Graham watched him silently, trying to detect a pattern.

"What have you got to dance about?" he asked. "Tell me. Forget I'm a reporter. I want to know."

"Talking to yourself, Gray," the photographer said grumpily behind him.

"Guess so," Graham said. "Looks like we'll have to grill the neighbours. God knows what rubbish we'll get out of them." His threat drew an expected blank.

The photographer's mobile rang and he was called to another job. "Gotta go," he said to Graham, "Bad car crash," and he was already retreating before Graham could call him back.

In the office that afternoon, Graham stared at his computer monitor, coffee cup clamped in both hands. He looked at the words he'd written. The first word, always in capital letters. The first sentence, never more than 25 words. The rules of the game. Had someone taught him the rules? Had he copied them from someone else? Or were the rules simply a legacy of journalism, passed down from one reporter, one newspaper, to the next? Here was another fatal road traffic accident. The story of three people, their life and death, in no more than 400 words. All rules successfully applied.

"An elegant example of the economy of language," Graham said to himself, immediately wondering whether he'd heard that phrase somewhere before.

He went to the bathroom. He passed rows of abandoned computers, each with screensavers playing endless animation to no-one. When he reached the urinal he already knew he couldn't go. He didn't want to. It was an excuse to get up and walk, to look at different walls. He stood in the centre of the room, watching himself in the mirror. He stepped forward, then back, then spun round as far as he could before losing his balance. He looked back at the mirror but the reflection was still the same.

He rang Karen's office but couldn't get past her secretary. He looked at the photo calendar on the wall but Miss September had nothing to say. The cursor on his screen blinked. He picked up a piece of paper and walked past the editor's office. He watched her through the glass – she was laughing down the phone, rocking in her chair. Had he dreamt of sitting in that chair once? He held up the piece of paper so she could see it and went through some double doors into advertising.

"Where's Cheryl?" he asked a dark-haired woman whose name he could never remember.

"Off sick," the woman replied.

"Oh." Graham realised the piece of paper he was holding was blank. He dropped it to his side before the woman could see. "What's wrong with her?"

"'Flu."

"Oh. I heard that's going round."

"Yes, it is."

"Start getting it a lot this time of year."

"Yes, you do."

The advertising department's walls were more interesting than editorial's. They were covered in charts and numbers. Mixed in were messages written in screaming marker pen: "Well done!" and "Needs improvement!" scattered among the numbers. Most of the computer monitors had little furry creatures with wobbly eyes. The dark-haired woman's had green fur. There was a fabric tag attached to it. "Happy Days!" it said.

101

Graham did a complete circuit of the building, the paper flapping in his hand like a kite struggling in the wind. He didn't really know anyone well enough to talk to them. They were just tops of heads, peeking above rows of computer monitors. He passed through reception, walking past a row of framed newspaper front pages on a wall above a sofa. Some of the splashes – the main story on the front page – were his. There had been a time when he'd take extra copies of those newspapers home, just so he could post them to relatives.

"Gray," the receptionist acknowledged brusquely as he went past.

Graham waved but there was nothing to say. When he got back to his desk he was glad that his phone was ringing.

"Got your message been in meetings all day sorry," Karen said in one, unpunctuated breath.

Graham didn't recall leaving a message. "Fancy takeaway for tea?"

"Takeaway's good. I'm going to be late again, I'm afraid. This damn case. Marcus wants me to go over the depositions one more…"

"Indian?"

"Er, yes. Indian. Great."

"Ring me when you're leaving and I'll order."

"Yes, thanks, good idea. Look, I'm sorry about these late nights."

Graham watched the cursor winking at him. "Can't be helped," he said.

Later that afternoon Brenda McMillan was telling her local councillor that unless the council made the road a 20 mile-an-hour zone outside Partridge Lane Primary School, a toddler was going to get hurt. Brian Trill, the local councillor, said that making a 20 mile-an-hour zone on Partridge Lane outside the primary school was a matter for the Highways Department and that, currently, it was not county council policy to have 20 mile-an-hour zones outside schools. Brenda McMillan said that wasn't good enough and she and other angry mums were going to organise a protest. Brenda and two other mums scowled suitably for their photograph. Around them was a small army of kids with beaming smiles and tongues sticking out.

Graham added a note to the end of the story and pressed send. Before technology had come along, filing a story had been a satisfyingly complex routine, like making fresh coffee. Now it left Graham with the feeling that something was missing.

Another click on the mouse delivered thirty emails. Drinks company launches new Smoothie – press release. House prices fall for the thirteenth month running, survey reveals. CBI calls for more home working. Increase your manhood to nine inches. School play announced, Gary Crisp to play Joseph, Unison response to nurses' pay deal, Website CMS package is the biggest and the best largest ever rice pudding breaks 100-year record cricket club goes homebrew bonkers new venue for rotary meeting injured cat…

"You got a minute?"

Graham blinked and looked over his shoulder. The photographer he'd asked to get some shots of the Dancing Man was standing behind him.

"Yes?"

"You still want a picture out at the social club?"

Graham saw the Dancing Man in his head. He twirls away until the photographer gets close to get a picture. Suddenly the Dancing Man stops, straightens his clothes and his hair, holds his head high and looks proudly into the camera lens.

"Yes," Graham said, trying to force the image away. "But leave it with me. I'll sort something, put something in the diary."

The photographer nodded and walked away.

Graham called on the Dancing Man on his way home. He was content just to watch from the car. The sun played on the social club wall, the honeyed light of an early autumn evening. The Dancing Man moved slowly, if not elegantly, while cars and pedestrians were just motion blurs, indistinct scratches on the surface. He thought about arranging the photograph. No rush, he thought. It didn't seem like the Dancing Man had plans to change his routine, to disappear.

He started to drive home but then changed his mind. He parked in the social club's car park. He hadn't been to any kind of club in years, and never to anywhere that promoted cabaret and karaoke. "Ugh, how cheap!" he could hear Karen saying. He thought of ringing her to say he would be late, but decided he didn't need to. She wouldn't be home yet anyway.

The club was a dour but somehow comforting place. It was one of the few places to survive the town's relentless regeneration programme. The walls were yellow from years of smoke. Beer mats were glued along one beam and plastic ashtrays were nailed to another. The seats, chairs and tables were a bric-a-brac of scratched wood and torn fabric. He sat on a barstool. A girl behind the bar put her nail file down, smiled at him and walked over.

"Do you know the Dancing Man...the guy outside?" Graham asked.

"Know of him," the girl said. "Why?"

"What do you know about him?"

The girl shrugged again. "What's to know? He's a

nutter. He scares the punters. I don't go near him, though. I live the other way."

"Where does *he* live?"

"Whatchoo wanna know for?"

Graham introduced himself. "No-one knows his name," he continued, "or where he lives. And he doesn't talk."

The girl seemed to have lost interest. "Well, you're the reporter. You tell us."

Graham felt frustrated. He grabbed a pen and scribbled a note: *If anyone knows anything, ask them to call me.*

On Sunday Graham went for a walk. Karen had gone to the office to work some more on the case, so there seemed little point staying at home. He wandered aimlessly around town, recognising and at the same time not recognising the place he grew up in. It was changing so fast. Buildings. People. He saw a wine bar, a place that had changed its name and appearance several times over the years. It had big windows and large leather sofas with low coffee tables between. In the days when he regularly drank there it was standing room only, with booming music and a carpet turned black with who knew what. Graham remembered it fondly.

He went in and flopped in a leather sofa. He didn't want a drink but was caught off guard when a girl came over to take his order. He looked over the shoulder of a suited man sitting in front of him, at the young girl he was chatting to. She was smiling flirtatiously at the man. The man was animated, talking rapidly.

The girl returned with Graham's drink. The man kept talking. Graham tried to block out his voice but couldn't. He ordered a second drink. The afternoon drifted.

"Hi," Graham said. "I'm a newspaper reporter. You

know what's really weird? I can chat all day to a mother who's just lost her son in a car accident, or has died from drugs, or has been beaten up...I can ask her all kinds of questions, and not fret about it one bit. But when I want to ask a beautiful girl for a dance, I can't. I lose my nerve."

The smile on the mouth he would kiss so many times widened. "Pity," Karen said.

Graham nodded. He opened his mouth to say something, hesitated, then shrugged. "See?"

"I do," Karen said.

Her eyes were green and brown, brown and green. They changed with the light, he learned, when he looked close enough, long enough.

"I do," she said.

Graham saw two empty glasses on the coffee table. Nothing left but fading froth.

He left the wine bar and walked on. He found himself approaching the social club and decided to call on the Dancing Man. He was there, his routine the same. The wind blew cold and hard off the sea and Graham could taste the salt in his mouth. The Dancing Man reached out towards the sea, arms mimicking the motion of the waves.

"Not such a good day for dancing," Graham said, bracing himself.

The Dancing Man's wispy hair seemed to wave with his hands.

"Good way to keep warm, though."

Just a few paving stones between them, his eyes fixed on his feet, Graham began to copy the Dancing Man's movements. Cars tooted. But they were motion blurs, scratches against the fiery sea.

"We can get banged up for this," Graham said. He smiled to himself.

Tap tap tap. Step forwards, twirl, back again. Graham found the rhythm almost immediately. "Have we been to the same dance school?" he asked.

The sun broke through the clouds and quietened him. A pause in the traffic. And for a fleeting moment Graham thought he heard music. Was it from the social club?

"I'd better go," he said, breaking his step. He turned to go but then faltered, looked back and eyed the Dancing Man carefully. "You're mad. I know you're mad, but I don't know why. I am going to find out."

The following week a boy shot himself in the head. There was a road rage incident on Arlington Road. A council meeting was held to decide which primary schools should close. A shopkeeper was fined £1,000 for selling alcohol to children. A hundred jobs were lost at a famous shoe factory. The football team lost 3-0 which all but ended their chances of automatic promotion. A five-year old was left home alone while the mother and father had a weekend in Scarborough. A scouts' sponsored walk raised £85 towards a new access ramp for their hut.

It was 30 minutes before deadline. Graham's fingers were poised over the keyboard. The cursor blinked expectantly. Caps lock on, ready for the first word. And then the first sentence. 25 words. What shall be today's tragedy?

Graham already knew. He'd known for a long time.

He typed a note for Karen. Then he grabbed his coat and drove to the social club. His mobile rang three times before he switched it off. He wound down the window and threw it at a bin as he drove past. It bounced off the side and smashed on the pavement. Somebody shouted.

The Dancing Man was nowhere to be seen. Graham leant on the steering wheel and stared through the windscreen.

Cars tooted as they went by. But they were little more than scratches on the surface. The sun came out from behind a cloud and flooded the pavement with a golden light. He felt its warmth. The sea hushed him, and the music started. *Step step step*, twirl, step forwards, *tap tap tap,* arms upwards, and back.

Phillip Dean Thomas

Phil Thomas writes fiction for adults. He lives in North Wales and works in public relations, creating articles for the media about business and its people. Discovering new and surprising things in the commonplace occupies his creative writing. Catch Phil's blog at www.wordcreative.co.uk.

Moving Magic

My name is Lucy Clements and I am twelve years old. Too old for fairy stories that's for sure. Or so I thought.

"Old enough to know better," Mum's always nagging. But often when there's something I want to do, I'm not old enough at all. At twelve you just can't win.

Take this move for instance. I don't want to go, but who cares? Dad's got himself a job, which is great; he's been unemployed for nearly a year. But guess where the job is? Ireland of all places. Why he applied there in the first place beats me. I told him he probably only got the job because no one wanted to go there, but he just laughed and swung me around.

"We'll have a good life there, Lu," he told me. I hadn't seen him that happy in a long while, but I couldn't laugh back.

You see, I like where I am. I like our house. And I love my room. I have the cutest wallpaper, all clouds and stars and stuff. Even thinking of leaving makes me want to cry, just lie down on my midnight-blue quilt and blub like a baby.

Mum and Dad only told me the other evening. We all sat around the kitchen table as if we were attending some important meeting and they said we were going to Ireland and that was that. Perhaps they didn't say it quite so bluntly, but that's what it boiled down to.

"Boiled down" is one of Mum's expressions. "Well it all boiled down to you not doing as you were told." Or "what it all boiled down to is you are under age." It boiled down to this, or it boiled down to that. Everything seems to boil down eventually, usually to something horrid.

Anyway, as Mum and Dad were describing our sudden life change, I began to feel really odd. Like I was made up of lots of fragments. One part of me wanted to throw up, another part wanted to run away, yet another part just wanted them to shut up. But the biggest part of all was simply boiling.

I wasn't boiling down. I was boiling mad. How dare they ruin my life like this. Then when Dad started prancing about trying to be funny, I just boiled over.

I flung my mug of tea at the wall and screamed and screamed. The cup smashed on impact and a brown splatter stain ran down the wall.

Dad looked shocked, but Mum grabbed me and held me close. Mum's trained to help people who are sad and worried but usually she never brings her work home. By the time she's spent all day sorting other people's problems the last thing she wants to do is listen to mine. But that evening, even after the screaming had stopped, she still held me for the longest time.

The next morning Mum asked if I wanted to stay home from school, but I said no. Time was running out, besides I didn't want to be with her.

Telling Frankie was as bad as I thought it would be. Frankie lives three doors down from me and she is my absolute best friend. She is so sweet. She has a lovely chocolate brown face, huge dark eyes with the whitest whites I've ever seen. And when they stare at you, you can tell what she's thinking. And when they look at me I know she really likes me and that I'm her best friend too.

Well, she cried and I cried, but thank goodness I didn't do any of that awful screaming again. Then we decided that we wouldn't go to school after all. I can't remember which of us suggested it first, but suddenly we had stopped crying and were giggling.

We wandered into town, which turned out to be a big mistake, because the first person we met was Mum.

"Hold it right there," she shouted. Like we were going anywhere, we were too shocked to move.

Within fifteen minutes we were at school and Mr Kemp, our headmaster, decided I should go home with Mum for the rest of the day, which seemed a pretty harsh punishment for half an hour up the town.

"Have you done that before?" Mum asked on the drive home. Her mouth was such a tight line she could barely get the words out.

"No."

She didn't seem to take much notice of my answer for she said. "I'm glad we're moving. That Frankie Mason is a bad influence on you," which was an unforgivable thing to say and I really hated her then.

Back home in my bedroom I slumped on my bed staring at the stars that Dad and I had carefully stencilled on the ceiling. Turning away from them, I squashed my face into my pillow and howled. I'd never felt so miserable. Suddenly I heard my name being called, well shouted actually.

"Lucy! Lucy, would you shut your noise?"

I lifted my face out of my pillow to see who was speaking and there standing by my bed was a tiny man dressed in a shabby green coat. His friendly face peered out from under the rim of a battered old hat. He was smiling and nodding in an encouraging sort of way and that was the moment I knew I was mad. Not boiling mad, or hopping mad. Just insane mad.

I was wondering what to do when he spoke again.

"Ah, sure Lucy love, things are never as black as you're painting them."

"Who…what… are you? What are you doing here?" I asked. My voice sounded shaky and weak, as if I had been ill for a long time.

He pulled off his hat, showing a mass of curly red hair, well frizzy orange really, and bowed. "O'Reilly. A leprechaun, who's a long way from home."

Now I maybe a bit day dreamy. Mum would say "there's no *maybe* about it." She's always telling me to get my head out of the clouds. But there's a big difference between the odd daydream about your favourite pop star and coming face to face with a leprechaun. But it seemed O'Reilly had his own reasons for visiting me.

"Lucy darling, I've come to beg a favour. Huge it is." He had tears in his eyes which he wiped away with the back of his hand. "I want you to take me home. Back to my lovely green, gorgeous Ireland."

A few days ago Ireland was just a coloured splurge in my geography book, now here was one of its most famous, mythical creatures, standing by my bed, asking me for help. It would be one crazy story to tell Frankie. I knew I should feel flattered, but somehow it just made me sad and all I could do was cry.

"Ah sure there's me crying because I want to go and you crying because you want to stay. We make an odd pair don't we darling?" He peered at me from under his bushy eyebrows. "What can I do to change your mind?"

Change my mind? Was he mad too? "There's nothing you can do." I yelled at him. "Nothing. I hate Ireland. I hate it. It's taking me away from everything I love. My school, my friends, Frankie…" I was gulping through tears that wouldn't stop. "Now see what you've done," I sobbed.

O'Reilly pulled a handkerchief from a black metal bucket-like container that was by his feet. "Wipe your eyes," he ordered. "Pretty eyes like them shouldn't be weeping."

I blew my nose and watched as O'Reilly rummaged

around in his strange bucket once more. "Let me show you what Ireland can give to you," he said, handing me a purple photo frame.

I had to look, even though part of me wanted to hurl it through the window. It had three slots for photographs.

The top picture was the three of us, Mum, Dad and me. I had never seen it before. We were in a park and it must have been winter because there was a Christmas tree all decorated in a little fenced off area. I was wearing a woolly hat and scarf and I couldn't stop staring at my face, it looked so different.

Mum seemed different too. Sort of soft. She was looking at me as if I was so precious, and I felt tears start to fill my eyes again.

"Ah Lucy love, you are precious," O'Reilly said, reading my mind. "But here your Mam never has enough time to show you."

Round one to the leprechaun.

The next photograph was a freckled-faced girl, with pig-tails. "Who is that?" I asked.

O'Reilly grinned. "That's Bridget Quiggly. She'll be just down the road from you, and she's lonely for a friend."

A friend I had yet to meet. How weird was that?

"I don't like the look of her." I said. I was determined to be difficult. Suddenly Bridget gave a shy grin and I nearly dropped the frame.

"She's moving!" Her smile was so nice I grinned back before I remembered I was supposed to dislike her.

The last photograph showed my bedroom. There it was complete with clouds and stars. But the edges of the picture were shimmering, you know, like when you stare into the distance on a hot, sunny day, everything wobbles slightly, well that's what the photo was doing. Slowly the scene shifted and I was staring into a different room.

"What's happening? Where's that?"

"That would be your bedroom in Ireland."

I so wanted to find something awful, but it was perfect. Enough moons and stars to fill my cosmic-loving heart to the brim.

The curtain rippled, moving to an Irish breeze I couldn't feel and into the picture ran a little dog. He tried to leap onto the bed but he was too small. He wouldn't give up though and he kept sort of bouncing. He looked so funny I wanted to hug him.

"That'll be your dog of course," O'Reilly told me. "Sure haven't you always wanted one?"

For the first time I tried to imagine a life in Ireland. I could hear Dad's voice in my head. "We'll have a good life there, Lu." Well, maybe we would.

Just then there was a tap on the door and before I could say "come in" or "hang on" O'Reilly vanished and Mum walked in. She always does that. Taps like she's being really polite, then barges in anyway. It really bugs me. This time though she just stood in the doorway. She had her "I'm going to give you a big lecture" face on. Or so I thought.

"Listen Lucy, I'm sorry for what I said about Frankie. I hope she comes and stays with us often, really I do."

Mum always does that. Turns things around. All my angry feelings sort of melted away and I ended up crying. Again.

Well, she hugged me and I hugged her back, until I felt something sharp sticking in me. It was the picture frame.

"Ooh, what's that?" Mum asked.

"Some photos."

"Let's have a look."

I gave her the frame and noticed the photographs had changed. They were all of me as a baby, ones I had seen before.

"Aw, you looked so cute." Mum said, and we spent the longest time chatting, which I suppose, boiled down to us liking one another's company.

After Mum had gone back downstairs, O'Reilly reappeared. "Wasn't that grand? Sure it's lucky you are."

"Yeah, well you're lucky too, seeing as you're coming to Ireland with us." I told him.

He started to skip around the room, laughing and crying at the same time. I have to say I knew how he felt. There was just one thing bugging me.

"O'Reilly, if you can do all this magic stuff, how come you can't get to Ireland on your own?"

"What? Cross that Irish Sea without company. Is it joking you are?" He lowered his voice and whispered. "I'll tell you a secret. You wouldn't catch me fishing, sailing or even drinking the stuff. I hate water!"

Funny how we've all got our own worries. Even leprechauns.

"I suppose I'll have to start packing soon." I said, looking around my room, there was so much to sort out.

"Pack indeed. Ah, there's plenty of time for that." O'Reilly pulled me to my feet. "Come on darling, let me show you the Irish jig," His eyes twinkled like two jewels. "Sure it all boils down to the footwork!"

Nurgish Watkins

Nurgish Watkins writes for children. She likes to focus on problems they might encounter, then throw some fantasy into the mix to add a bit of sparkle to the ordinary.

Choices

"If you don't mind just taking a seat for a few minutes, someone will come to you. They're expecting you. Would you like a coffee?"

Joe returned the receptionist's smile and shook his head. "No, I'll be fine thanks; I had a drink in town before I got here." He sat on the edge of the comfortable seat in the foyer, and tried desperately to relax. It took a conscious effort to stop fiddling with his cuffs, his watch, his mobile; and sitting still didn't come naturally – he was a fidget at the best of times. He wore a dark warm and expensive jacket, fairly new black jeans and the grey jumper Jackie had bought him for his birthday.

"It's got cashmere in it," she had told him, her eyes shining, her expression eager to please, and loving.

I'm a lucky, lucky man, thought Joe.

Even that thought didn't help his nerves at this moment though. He looked around him for distraction. Two boys were at reception now, chatting to the girl. The stocky, dark-haired one laughed as he showed her a couple of DVDs, and asked her for the key to the TV lounge. "Go on, you know I'm a good lad, I'll bring it back," The receptionist smiled doubtfully as she handed over a key, "Thanks, babe", he said, pocketing it. Mmm, thought Joe far too cocky, for the circumstances. He pulled himself up sharply. Who was he, Joe, to judge? The boy was entitled to his defence mechanism; and Joe knew better than most, how cocky can be just a cover for inadequacy. Both boys turned to go. The other lad, fair and skinny had a lot of spots made more noticeable by his pallor. There was a little boy look in the curve of his cheek and the way his hair stuck out a bit at the back. The anxious expression on his face smote Joe's heart. He looked poorly nourished; and not just physically. There was an almost unfinished raw look about him; vulnerability. *I don't think you've known much love or care,* thought Joe.

And I bet he's easily-led, thought Joe, glancing at the other boy, *and the chances are,* he thought, *that you are not the best of company for him.*

He looked away from the lads, and around at his surroundings. Someone had obviously made an effort with the Christmas decorations; a tree twinkled in the corner; a real tree; Joe had caught a whiff of that evocative heavy evergreen smell as he had walked to his seat. The whole place looked bright; as if decorated with a deliberate cheeriness; an upbeat message was being flashed to the lads and to any visitors. Then Joe saw the very obviously home-made crib in the other corner; its simplicity in stark, but actually pleasing contrast to the glitter and tinsel.

"Can you just sit there for a few minutes; somebody will come out and take your details shortly – they are all a bit busy". Young Joe had been so happy to get inside.

It had been bitterly cold; and another night under the bridge or in the doorway of the new superstore had been beyond him.

"You'll get used to it," one of the others had said to him, on his first night.

Get used to it! Joe had read somewhere that the average life expectancy of a homeless person was the early forties. A woman dispensing soup and rolls had come out of the van to speak to him. "There is a hostel you can go to tonight, a decent place, better than most. Go up Prince's Street and half way up on the right hand side you will come to a little side-street. At the top of this you'll find the place. It is known as Marty's, I think the proper name is St Martin's." Her voice had been urgent. It was like she was really trying to save him, or something.

Maybe she had looked at him and thought he wasn't a completely lost cause. She even came again to talk to him again, just before they drove their van away. He was huddled with the polystyrene cup held close to his chest, trying to soak up the warmth.

"Get off the streets, Joe, before you begin to go the same way as them". Her voice was low and she nodded in the direction of the group of men and the few women.

"I am like them," he had half-whispered. He was wary of the others' reaction to his being singled out like this. It might be crazy, but he didn't want the group to think he was trying to be better than them. After all, they had in their way accepted him; and not asked too many question.

"No, you're not," she said fiercely. "But you soon will be."

He knew what she meant. Of course he did. Despite all the times he had been told he was stupid, Joe knew that he wasn't. As yet he hadn't dulled the pain with alcohol or drugs, and that did make him different. From what he had seen so far, Joe reckoned that addiction of one sort or another, was reason most of the others were homeless. But he still understood what the woman was getting at. Maybe the homelessness sometimes led to the addiction, not the other way round.

A friendly youngish bloke had led him to a sort of dormitory, and advised him to keep his possession close to him, or hand them in for safe-keeping. Well, that didn't present him with a problem. Joe had taken virtually nothing with him, when he had left home; a few clothes, his walkman and a few tapes. His rucksack now held only a load of laundry and a couple of books.

Jamie, the hostel volunteer, had led him to some sort of common room where a couple of lads were lazily play-

ing pool, with a couple of others sprawled in front of the television. "I'll leave you to settle in; get to know some of the other lads". Joe nodded, terrified. Jamie must have seen his fear. "You'll be fine. Supper's at eight; the others will show you the dining-hall. And Joe…" Joe looked up at him. "In the morning, if you come to the office at ten, a key-worker, Anna will talk to you." "Right," Joe replied. He had no idea what a key-worker was. Joe wondered how on earth he was going to actually get to ten the next morning. He felt hemmed in and lost all at the same time. In some strange way this was worse than the street.

"Got any fags?" one of the pool players asked.

"No, sorry," he answered. "Where you from then?"

The other lad looked up from chalking his cue.

"Stoke" Joe replied.

He seemed to have forgotten how to make conversation. Is this what three weeks on the street had done to him?

"Oh, my uncle comes from Stoke", the first youth said. "Who do you support, then…Port Vale or Stoke?"

"Port Vale," Joe replied, saying a silent prayer that he had given the "right" answer.

Apparently, he had. "Want a game? Play the winner?"

Joe had nodded. It would pass a bit of time. Take his mind off food – another couple of hours until the evening meal; then, eventually to be able to go to bed. It would be good to lie down; to be able to wash, to be warm.

But, he couldn't sleep. His mind raced. This was the worse he had felt since he had banged the door of home behind him, with thoughts only of getting away. It wasn't that she was a terrible person; he hadn't been abused. He had heard and read enough to know that others were far worse off than him. In fact, she was more to be pitied than blamed. She had had him fairly young, and had no support, not from her parents nor least of all from his long-vanished father. She had cared for him...most of the time; fed him, even played with him, when he was small. No, it was what she did to herself that Joe couldn't live with...not any more.

There were parties; excesses; but it wasn't even that. It was the disastrous lurching from one relationship to the next. There had been Simon who had been scary, really scary – Joe had a memory of fleeing to a refuge in the middle of the night, after he and his mum had been locked out of the house.

After that, there had been a guy called Tony, who had been fine to start with, but turned out to be seriously into pubs and betting shops, and there had been no money for food. Then there had been....Joe pulled the pillow over his head in an effort to forget. It was only recently really that Joe had begun to see the pattern. His mum would be down, needing his company, calling friends late at night, going to the off-licence every evening after work. The nights out with the girls would start. Then would come the excitement; the exhilarated mood, and the man's name would be dropped more and more frequently into conversation.

"He's really nice, Joe, really takes care of me; he's got a good job; he's different; you'll like him".

Hints would be dropped about Joe meeting this guy; elaborate plans made for how they might all move in together. Carl, the last one had been called. Joe hadn't hung around to meet him. He had had enough. He was seventeen, not some little kid to be placated by trips to the football. He wasn't going to be the shadow figure in his mother's big soap opera life anymore. And most of all, he wasn't going to be there to pick up the pieces when it all went wrong...hug her, tell her she would always have him, ring in sick for her when she couldn't face going to work...All of it – the whole pattern – enough.

He missed her, of course he did; she must be worried. But he didn't know how to make contact without a whole big fuss. Had she contacted the police? He had left a note, not saying much really, just the usual stuff about getting in touch. Alex, his best friend would be worried. Joe had come near to telling him, but knew that Alex would have tried to stop him from running away. Alex and his sensible grown-up parents; they had always been good to Joe too, never seemed to look down on him or his mum, as some of his classmates had. In fact there were times when he had sat in Alex's kitchen waiting for him; talking to Mrs Peters, when he had actually felt safe – that the world didn't have to be such a chaotic place.

Eventually, he had slept, heavy exhausted strange sleep. His heart had been pounding as he woke suddenly, and he felt a few seconds of complete panic. What was he doing here?

He heard noises; someone was snoring, somebody else was mumbling in an agitated way, in his sleep. Then something happened to Joe. There had been a distant sound of music being played; he thought he could just make out the tune of 'Silent Night', but it wasn't just that. Someone had left the curtain half-open, and he could see a star, really bright. He tried to remember some prayers – his mother had gone through a religious phase when Joe had been about seven. In the end, he had just silently asked for help, for some direction. With real clarity, he became aware that he stood at a crossroads; that the choice he made now would determine everything.

It may have been a moment of epiphany, but of course life is messy and his troubles didn't end there. But

121

there had been a new determination about Joe. He would go back; he knew he was lucky; that for many of the home-less that was not an option. Whatever it took, he would leave home the next time, in the right way. And he was smart enough to know that meant education and qualifica-tions. And his mother...well, Joe knew that she wasn't go-ing to change. He would somehow have to react differently; not let it get to him quite so much. And talk to Mrs Peters; that would help.

A smiling middle-aged man came, now to Joe; his hand outstretched. "The lads are waiting for you in the hall, Dr Hayes. It is so good of you to come and talk to them, again; I can't tell you how much the last lot enjoyed listening to you. We can talk to them until we're blue in the face, but it makes all the difference in the world, to hear from someone who once stood in their shoes".

Joe smiled, stood up and shook hands. As he fol-lowed the man out of the foyer, he looked once more at the homemade crib in the corner of the foyer.

Noreen Wainwright

Noreen Wainwright is Irish, but lives with her husband, a dairy farmer, in the Staffordshire Moorlands. Farming life has in-spired many of her articles. She teaches part-time at Newcastle-under-Lyme college, and also day-dreams about being a crime writer. She has co-written a non-fiction book, which has a re-lated blog: www.thehomelyyear.blog.co.uk.

The Keeper's Keeper

As Tom walked along the pathway for the last time that day, he was certain Rita would be there. She'd become a regular fixture in Victoria Park of late, and always sat on one particular bench. A strange old dear, certainly, but always friendly.

Sixty-odd he guessed, and overweight, she usually had a roll-up in one hand and a small bottle of mineral water in the other. At least, the bottle would originally have contained water. These days, Tom suspected, it was almost certainly neat gin or vodka. The most outrageous makeup (almost theatrical, Tom felt), and violent red hair with grey showing at the roots, meant Rita could never be overlooked, or ignored. Where, or how, she lived was anyone's guess. She never discussed it.

"Isn't it time you were going home, Rita?" he called out as he drew level. "You'll freeze to death if you sit there much longer."

"Impossible, dear," she answered. "And as for 'home', don't make me laugh!" She took a swig from the ever-present bottle, and Tom wondered how on earth she could afford its contents. "Besides, we need a chat," she continued. "Take a pew. And don't worry, I don't bite, unless the need arises!"

Tom joined her on the bench. "Not for too long, mind... You might not feel the cold, but I do. Never used to, but these days…"

"These days you don't have a hut to hide in when it's cold," Rita interjected, "since it was burnt down. Still, won't matter soon, will it? The park's gone right down the pan, the Council's sick of it, and if they close it you'll be out of a job."

"You obviously read the local rag," he commented,

somewhat surprised that Rita should know, or even care, about local issues. She was right, of course. Vandalism, under-funding and simple neglect, had reduced Victoria Park to a sad reflection of the beautiful oasis it once was. Families were reluctant to come here these days. The local Council, weary of the problems, was also seeking ways to cut its budget. There were rumours that the park might even be closed for good. It was unthinkable, but Tom was saddened and relieved in equal measure. At his age it was all too much to cope with.

"Never read newspapers," Rita admitted. "Far too depressing. But I know all about Victoria Park. What I don't know is why, since you've been keeper here for twenty years, you're happy to stand by and do absolutely *nothing* to help. I've been watching you for weeks now, hoping you'd show some fight, some spirit." She shook her head. "Frankly Tom, I'm disappointed in you."

Tom was speechless for a moment, because the last thing he'd expected was a lecture. On the other hand, she wasn't the first person to challenge him on the deterioration of the park, and probably wouldn't be the last. "Er, hang on a minute!" he objected. "*Watching* me? I'm only the humble keeper here, not the Council treasurer. Like it or not there's absolutely nothing I *can* do. I mean, what kind of superhuman powers do you think I've got?"

"More than you know, dear." She drew on her roll-up, then exhaled a great cloud of smoke. "Actually there's a lot you can do. Get a campaign going, for starters, and involve the whole town! Get everyone to bombard the Council, the local MP, the newspapers, with letters of protest. Don't forget local radio and TV – they love all that conflict! But you'll have to look smart. The Council meeting about these budget cuts is only weeks away, and if necessary you might even organize a protest for that day, with as many people there as you can get. Banners, placards, local press, media, the lot!"

She paused to take another sip from the bottle, before giving way to a violent fit of coughing. She looked suddenly ill and frail. How much longer, he worried, would her body tolerate this treatment? As for this hair-brained scheme of hers, it was clearly nothing more than the ramblings of a sick and lonely old lady. What did she know about local politics, and the mysterious workings of the town Council?

"Rita, you must know how impossible all that is!" he protested mildly.

"A lot of work, yes," she granted. "Impossible, no. You'll have to get the Council on side of course, convince them you're serious, *and* committed. But saving the park from closure is only the start," she stressed, clearly warming to the topic. "It'll still look like a rubbish dump, so you'll probably need to form some sort of committee, so funds can be raised to fix it all up."

Her face instantly lit up as a new thought struck her. "I know, how about asking for local volunteers to come and help out as well? Children, even, to help plant things? They'll come in droves once the campaign gets going. You can do it, Tom! Trust me!"

She fell silent for a moment, studying his face intently, as though challenging him to come up with further objections. She puffed quietly on her roll-up.

"I just don't get it," he said at last. "How come you've got all these fancy ideas?" He laughed suddenly at the absurdity of it all. "It's a wind-up, right? No offence Rita, but you're the last person…"

"Yes, I know," she interrupted wearily. "No-one expects words of wisdom from a broken-down, drunken old lady, do they?" She smiled wistfully. "It's a pity you didn't know me when I was young. Blonde, and beautiful, people said, with a smashing figure. I was on the stage, you know, and quite famous in my time. Wasn't plain old Rita then, of course. No, I was Margarita Manning then, and a star turn! A bit of singing, a bit of dancing, a bit of comedy thrown in…" She chuckled wickedly. "And all of it a bit saucy, if you follow me!"

Tom couldn't imagine it for a minute, because the years hadn't been kind to Margarita Manning. The name meant nothing to him either, and at fifty-five he wasn't that much younger than Rita was. Virtually the same generation. If the story was true, it was probably some obscure provincial theatre where once Margarita Manning had trodden the boards.

She started rambling again. "What times they were… Handsome young men fighting over me at the stage doors…taken to supper clubs and nightclubs…showered with gifts…endless marriage proposals. You won't believe it, dear," she said dreamily, "but they all worshipped at my feet."

Tom shivered slightly. The crisp autumn day was already dissolving into early dusk. The sky was clear and bright, which probably meant a sprinkling of frost overnight. He glanced discreetly at his watch. This conversation could go on for ages, and it was growing colder by the minute. It didn't seem to be troubling Rita though, who looked all set for a lengthy reminiscence about past glories and romantic conquests.

But Rita, clearly noting the gesture, said, "Don't worry, dear, I'm not going to bore you to death. I was just making the point that I wasn't always old and decrepit, but never mind that now." She stabbed a grubby finger in his direction. "What's important is Victoria Park, and you've got to fight for it. And it *is* important, not just for you but the whole local community."

"You're a strange lady, Rita," Tom said bluntly. "I mean, why should you care?" Was she even a local woman? He'd never seen her around until fairly recently. And with that hair she wasn't exactly invisible! "It isn't your problem, after all."

"I played in this park as a nipper," she sighed. "It was beautiful then, and I've still got some precious memories of it. That's why I care, and so should you. It's *everyone's* problem, including yours, and I'm only trying to help." She broke into a wide grin, displaying teeth the colour of burnt ochre. Her tone became playful and mischievous. "Might even be your guardian angel for all you know!"

Tom rose stiffly to his feet. "You know, you should definitely go easier on that mineral water! Come on, I'll walk you to the exit."

They strolled in easy silence to the east gate. Just beyond that was the car park. "Can I give you a lift anywhere?" he offered. "It's no trouble."

She shook her head. "No, dear, I don't have to go very far." She started to walk away then paused, and looked back. "You won't forget what I've said about this park, will you? It's important, Tom."

* * *

The current committee meeting finally drew to a close. And perhaps for the first time, Tom, its chairman, was allowing himself to feel quietly optimistic. Nothing was certain yet, he realized, but the signs were good. Above all he couldn't believe how lucky he'd been. He'd started tentatively enough, with letters to the local paper. These were followed by nervous approaches to his immediate employers, the Parks and Gardens Department, with a general

127

outline of Rita's proposals. What he hadn't anticipated was how deeply people felt about the fate of the park, and how eager everyone suddenly was to contribute to its resurrection. The whole campaign, from small beginnings, seemed to gather a momentum of its own, and without even the need for public protest.

The Council was now reviewing the situation. Grant applications had been made to several sources, including the Lottery. And he had more offers from local volunteers than he knew what to do with. Perhaps more importantly, the local paper was backing the campaign to the hilt, giving it essential publicity, and whipping the town into a frenzy of enthusiasm.

And yet, Tom acknowledged, it was Rita to whom the whole town owed a huge debt of gratitude, and his dearest wish would be to tell her so. The trouble was that she was now nowhere to be seen, and what concerned him above all was the state of her health. Phone calls to the local hospital, and even the Social Services, had revealed nothing. His greatest hope was that she had close relatives, even though she'd never mentioned them, who were perhaps taking care of her somewhere.

Tom and Jack, a fellow committee member, were the last to leave the meeting room that evening. "I managed to find that info you asked me to search for, on the internet," Jack said, handing Tom the printed A4 sheets, "on Margarita Manning. It's riveting stuff, but it makes no sense to me. See what you think."

Tom sat down again, growing more puzzled by the minute as he read through the printouts. Jack was right, it didn't make any sense at all. This woman was born in 1880. By 1897 she was already performing in Music Halls, and went on to become a big Music Hall star. There were two disastrous marriages and a string of affairs. Even more astonishing was that, in her heyday, she was earning £200 a week. She died in 1945, from an alcohol-related illness, at the age of sixty-five.

"Quite a girl wasn't she!" Jack said. "She's the only Margarita Manning I could find with anything like the right profile. And it all seems to fit, except it can't be your Rita."

"Obviously not," Tom agreed, still deep in thought. "But Rita was in a world of her own half the time. Who knows? Margarita Manning could even have been her grandmother, or a great aunt, so Rita would know all about her. Maybe Margarita led the sort of life that Rita always wanted and never achieved. She's probably been telling this tale for so long she actually believes it herself! Either that or she was just having a laugh!"

"But why?" Jack persisted. "Isn't it all a bit weird, claiming to be someone who died sixty three years ago?"

"It's certainly eccentric," Tom conceded, "but that's Rita in a nutshell – a bit eccentric. She even muttered something about guardian angels at one stage! Mind you, she'd been knocking back the old 'mineral water' like no-body's business, at the time. But let's not forget," he added, feeling suddenly disloyal, "that it was Rita who dreamed up this whole campaign thing, not me. So if she's invented a few fantasies for herself, who are we to criticise?"

"Fair comment," Jack acknowledged. "From the sounds of it that's probably all she's got left now, just fantasies." He looked at his watch. "Fancy a beer on the way home? My shout?"

On the other side of the room, unseen and paying close attention, Rita smiled with satisfaction as she watched them leave. Victoria Park was now in good hands. Job done.

Joyce Hicks

Joyce Hicks has been writing short stories for nearly 20 years, many of which have been published in national women's magazines. She has been a finalist, or short-listed, in quite a few short story competitions. For eleven years she was Chair of her local writers' circle.

Slight Expectations

The author stood in St James's churchyard close to the village of Cooling in Kent. He could feel a soft May breeze on his face, he could smell the sweet odour of early roses, he could hear the faint hum of insects in the dry air, and his mouth retained the bitter taste of the tablet he'd forgotten to take with lunch and had just had to swallow dry. He could see nothing because he could not see.

"Why on earth do you want to stay here, Gerald?" his wife had demanded, impatience being such a natural mood with her that he scarcely even registered it any more. "The church has been here for centuries, it'll still be here next time we come."

"Not necessarily," he'd replied, hoping his measured tone would conceal the oppressive gloom he felt. "You know how little planning officers care about heritage or the environment. If any big business comes along wanting to build a factory or retail park, and it isn't averse to forking out a few backhanders to the right people, then nowhere in the country is safe."

"Oh, not planning officers again," his wife had sighed. "If it's not them, it's oil companies, if it's not them it's politicians or civil servants or anyone who's ever had anything to do with the bloody government, and if it's none of them, it's car dealers. Don't you ever give up?" He knew what was coming, and it did, word for word. "You've wasted your life fighting for lost causes, and half of mine too."

"Those bastards could've killed Lynsey with that mobile death trap they sold her," he'd said, teeth clenching. Lynsey was their daughter who now lived in Bronte country up in Yorkshire somewhere. She wouldn't speak to her father any more, although she'd never exactly said why. "They're crooks and morons, the whole lot of them, and the best thing I ever did was getting them closed down."

"Being crooks and morons is the job description for second-hand car dealers," Jennifer had said. It was the closest she ever came to agreeing with him about anything these days. "So you're determined to waste an hour here 'drinking in the atmosphere'?"

"What is this life..." he'd begun.

"OK, then I'm going to find a shop and get some food to take home for dinner. We've got a long drive and I want to get started as soon as possible. Will you be all right on your own for a bit?"

Gerald had nodded, assuming she was looking at him, and listened while she strode across the dry grass, the wooden buttons of her long cashmere cardigan clacking against headstones as she brushed unfeelingly past them. Their old Morris Minor had coughed unhappily to life, then given a parting whine of complaint as Jennifer had steered it off the embankment onto the tarmac lane, and driven out of earshot.

Then there was peace, perfect peace. It might only last a short time, but for that short time Gerald hoped to have what he craved, what he'd yearned for ever since he'd been young and fiery and had begun to fight against the injustices of the world. Likening himself to a modern day Don Quixote, and oblivious to the irony of that comparison, he had taken up arms against corporate bullies and municipal incompetents, greasy palmed potentates in local and national government, self-serving swindlers running businesses throughout the length and breadth of England's once green and pleasant land. Sometimes it seemed to him that his life had been one unending battle, and one in which the few small victories were mightily outweighed by what they had cost. His health was gone, his daughter was gone, his few friends had long since started to treat him as a figure of fun, and his wife seemed scarcely to tolerate his existence.

Some small flying creature brushed against his face and he waved his hand to deter it from landing on him. Suddenly, he felt lonely and helpless: a writer who could not see to write any more, standing in the graveyard where 'Great Expectations' had begun, with no expectations, great or otherwise, left to him anymore. "What would you do, Boz?" he murmured aloud. "You never gave up. How can I imitate The Inimitable?"

There was a rustling of dry grass which he wasn't sure could be attributed to the wind. "Is someone there?" he asked. "Is that you, Jennifer?" He knew it could not be her, for he would have heard the car return, but wanted to give the impression that he was not alone.

"My apologies, sir," came an animated voice. "It was not my intention to disturb you. I come here sometimes to relive my past, but there is rarely anyone else present."

Gerald turned to face the direction the voice came from. "That's all right," he said, affecting an air of bonhomie. "It's a free country."

"I am pleased you think so, sir," said the stranger. "Might I enquire what draws you to such a desolate spot as this?"

Gerald smiled ruefully. "Much like you, I am reliving my past," he said.

"Indeed? You are a Kentish man then – or a man of Kent?"

"Neither. I was born and bred in St Ives in Cornwall. But I was a writer of some repute, and now that I can no longer follow that profession, I spend as much time as I can manage visiting places with literary associations. My wife is very obliging in that respect." The newcomer said nothing, so Gerald felt constrained to keep talking to fill the uncomfortable silence. "I lost my eyesight a couple of years ago.

Diabetes. My own fault – I didn't do what the doctors said and I've paid the price."

"My condolences, sir," said the stranger, seeming genuinely saddened.

Gerald warmed to him, instinctively feeling that he was someone who was genuinely interested in other people. "Did you know this churchyard is supposed to have inspired Dickens when he wrote the opening scene of 'Great Expectations'?" he said, glad of an opportunity to demonstrate his knowledge. He gestured with his hand, vaguely, as he had slightly lost his bearings and could not remember exactly where to point. "Those little headstones there are referred to in the book, although he changed the number to suit his requirements."

"I am flattered, sir, that you are so familiar with my work," said the stranger. "I am the humble author to whom you refer. Charles John Huffam Dickens at your service."

Gerald held his breath for a moment. Either he or the stranger were mad, and at that moment he felt it was more likely to be himself. But if one were going to meet the ghost of Charles Dickens, he reasoned, where more probable than in a place so closely associated with him. Perhaps he had summoned it with his recent incantation. He could not run away, and the newcomer had been harmless enough up to then, so perhaps the best thing was to continue their conversation as if the encounter were the most normal thing in the world. If it were the newcomer who was insane, then humouring him might be the wisest course of action. And if it were not – well, what difference did it make what he did.

"I believe I am well loved in this area still," said Dickens, as if somehow aware that Gerald had reached the end of his train of thought.

"I don't know about 'loved'," Gerald said, as coolly as if he were chatting to his agent about a new book proposal.

"The tourist people here trade on your name like nobody's business, but hopefully there's still a few people more interested in your work than in tatty memorabilia."

"It is something to be remembered, nevertheless," said Dickens ruefully, "whether by tradesmen or by the more learned."

His charismatic voice seemed to glide from emotion to emotion like a skilled musician playing scales upon a particularly haunting and beautiful instrument. Gerald thought he could listen to him for hours. "You're certainly the area's biggest draw," he said ingratiatingly, beginning to enjoy the bizarre exchange, and even more anxious than before to parade his literary credentials. "Even though there are many other writers with links here. William Cobbett was in the military garrison in Chatham for a few months. Jane Austen's brother lived near Canterbury. Samuel Pepys often came down here to the Dockyard on business. Kipling, Waugh, Wells – oh, too many to list."

"I do not know the last three," said Dickens. "You seem extremely erudite on these matters."

Gerald sighed. "Escapism, I suppose," he said. "Reading took me away from the real world."

"Is your real world so dreadful then?" Dickens asked.

Gerald put his hand out, feeling for a headstone and silently cursing that he'd left his white stick in the car. Eventually his fingers touched cold granite, and he moved to rest against it, hoping he was not desecrating a grave with which his unusual companion had a connection. "It is for me," he admitted after a moment's thought. "I see so much corruption and injustice everywhere. I've spent my life fighting it, in my own small way, but it suddenly seems so futile. What good can one voice do?" He had long known that he needed to unburden himself to somebody, and the ghost or madman, whichever it was, would serve that purpose far better than anyone who actually knew him. Whatever he said, he was sure it would go no further.

The rustling grass which had signalled Dickens' arrival came to his ears again, and Gerald guessed he was moving. He felt his heart speed up, and his hand curled into a fist by his side. If the newcomer were going to harm him after all, he decided, he would do whatever he could to defend himself. But when Dickens spoke again, he was no closer than before. "It is the duty of every free man to speak up for what they believe to be right," he said, his voice having taken on a fervour which was wholly enthralling. "I railed against exactly those foul stains upon the whitened sepulchre of our society that you speak of, and it cost me more than you can imagine. But I would not take back a word that I spoke nor a line that I wrote, if it gave me twenty more years of healthy life. Evils flourish when they are allowed to grow unchecked -- even one voice can play its part in holding them back."

"That's easy for you to say," Gerald replied, feeling resentful. "You need money nowadays to undertake proper opposition strategies to any sort of major injustice, and my money came from writing novels. I'm blind now, in case I hadn't mentioned it!"

"That must be a cruel burden to bear indeed," said Dickens, his voice quieter. "But surely it is not beyond your means to employ some amanuensis, some clerk who could take down your words as you spoke them?"

Gerald smiled bitterly, thinking of the expensive voice recognition software which Jennifer had arranged to be installed on his computer before he came home from the hospital, and which he had never even tried to use. "It's not that easy," he said. Then, unable to ignore the weakness of his own assertion, continued, "besides, even if I wrote more books and earned enough to fund new projects, what use would a blind man be at a rally or leading a meeting?" Even as he spoke, he knew he was talking nonsense; the same nonsense he'd been telling himself and others since he'd lost his sight. Had he just been seeking an excuse to give it all up, and blindness had given him what he wanted? Perhaps he had brought the affliction upon himself deliberately?

"Your writing and your fighting are separate activities then?" asked Dickens.

Gerald nodded. "Of course," he said. "I use – I used – my earnings from books to fund what I really cared about."

"You are familiar with my novels?" Dickens asked. Gerald nodded, and Dickens continued, "then you will have read 'Oliver Twist', 'Bleak House', 'Hard Times' …"

"I've read every novel you wrote", Gerald told him, "and all the short stories. Several times."

"And what are they about?" Dickens asked. "What is "Oliver Twist" about?"

Gerald shook his head disdainfully. "It's about an orphan who falls into bad company …"

Before Gerald could develop his polished précis of the plot, Dickens interrupted. "'Oliver Twist' is about the inhumane treatment of the poor by local and national institutions, 'Bleak House' is about corruption and incompetence in government and the law, 'Hard Times' is about a philosophy that regards men as no more than machines to be used in factories until they wear out. Should I continue?"

Gerald felt the ever-present unhappiness which had gnawed at him for years start to falter. "Of course," he said slowly. "Exactly the sorts of injustice and hypocrisy I fought against myself. But that was something apart from my literary work. I thought little of my novels because my heart was in the eternal battle and I wrote merely to pay the bills. But you seem to be suggesting that my novels should have <u>been</u> my battle? Pens and swords, and all that?"

137

"There are few ways more efficacious to right a wrong than to hold that wrong up to the light, so that everyone can see it. A good writer can do that better than anyone else. Mock the perpetrators or recount the tragic stories of their victims, in fiction as well as in fact, and public opinion will do what your one voice alone cannot."

"Yes!" Gerald had grown suddenly excited, standing free from the headstone against which he had leant and rocking back and forth as his mind whirled with new ideas and plans. "I can still fight and I can still write. It's the same thing. It's so obvious. Why didn't I think of it years ago! How much good I could have done. But there's time yet. I can still make a mark. Thank you, Mr Dickens, thank you so much. I feel just like Scrooge waking up after the spirits have been!" He stretched out his hand to shake that of the man who had helped him to see, but froze, interrupted by the familiar sound of his car pulling up by the churchyard wall. "Ah, my wife's back. I want to tell her what you said. She'll be so pleased. Or you could tell her yourself. Would you mind? I'm sorry – I didn't introduce myself …"

"Who are you talking to?" Jennifer asked, her heavy feet crushing twigs beneath them as she half ran towards him. "Are you all right? I wasn't long."

"Better than ever," Gerald announced, grinning like an idiot. "Mr Dickens here has just been encouraging me to keep fighting the good fight. He showed me where I've been going wrong all these years, and how I can carry on, eyes or no eyes. Didn't you?" He tilted his head, straining to hear something which would enable him to look in the right direction.

"There's no-one here," Jennifer said, tensely. "You must have been daydreaming."

Gerald took a step towards her. He felt the soft May breeze on his face, he smelled the sweet odour of early roses, he heard the faint hum of insects in the dry air; but the bitter tablet taste in his mouth had gone. "I have been dreaming," he told her. "For a long time. But at last I'm awake."

Michael O' Connor

Michael O'Connor's fiction has appeared in many UK/North American print and online magazines, and Urban Fox Press published a book of his short stories entitled 'Where Do They All Belong?' His non-fiction book 'From Chaucer to Childish: Writers and Artists in the Medway Towns' is available from Medway Delta Press.

Please, Don't Call Me Herbie

This isn't one of those clever stories with a twist ending, so I'll come clean straightaway.

My name's Gertie and I'm a car; an old Volkswagen Beetle to be precise. And before you jump to any conclusions, any resemblance to a certain Herbie, otherwise known as the Love Bug, is purely coincidental.

Unlike him, I can't fly, or swim underwater, or do lots of clever tricks, but we do have one thing in common; owners who need a push start with their love lives. Take mine. Susan had been on her own for three years, ever since Patrick passed away.

I was his pride and joy, which explains why Susan didn't want to part with me, even though I'm not in the first flush of youth. It didn't even cross her mind to get a new car, at least it hadn't until six weeks ago. Now, it's all changed. She's met a man, thinks she likes him because he's so very different from Patrick. I'm worried in case it gets serious.

Don't misunderstand me. I want Susan to be happy. She's only forty-four, she deserves to have a man in her life, so long as it isn't this one.

What's wrong with him? How long have you got. The worse thing is that he keeps telling Susan she should 'move with the times' which translated means, scrap yours truly, and get some new wheels.

There's a limit to what I can do. I haven't got air conditioning, or even a sun roof. I was becoming resigned to my fate when one day something happened which gave me fresh hope.

I got a flat tyre.

I didn't do it on purpose. It was just one of those things. Susan called out the AA. I mean she could have mended it herself, but having just written out a cheque for a year's membership….

The man they sent out was just perfect. His first words were "what a great little car. And in such lovely condition."

As he worked, he told Susan his name was Michael. He said she could ask for him if she had any more trouble. Well I fell for him immediately. He wasn't the type of man that would run to the dealers and have me traded in, and even I could see how much he fancied Susan. I sat back and waited for nature to take its course. Only it didn't. Susan hardly noticed him.

Luckily he wasn't so easily put off. "Are you married?" he asked her.

"No" she said, a bit hesitantly.

"Only I'd love to take you out to dinner sometime."

"Oh," she said, "thank you for asking, but I'm really not interested."

Not interested. How could she say that? He was charming, good looking in a rugged but approachable way. He obviously had great taste too, after all, he liked me, now didn't he? So that's when I decided to try and help things along.

It hasn't been easy arranging little problems, as I said, I'm not Herbie, but last week when Susan was on her way to see HIM, I managed to make the fuel gauge stick on half full, even though we were fast running out. I found somewhere safe, gave a few coughs and splutters and came to a full stop.

"What's wrong, Gertie?" she said as she stared at the fuel gauge and willed me to move, but I wasn't going anywhere.

Out came the AA. Luckily for me it was Michael again.

"Good evening, Mrs Peters," he said, which was impressive. I mean he'd only seen her membership card once. "How lovely to see you."

"What do you mean?" she said, staring at him as if he was mad. "How can it be lovely when I'm stuck here?"

He laughed. "So what's wrong?"

"I'm not sure. It feels like we ran out of fuel."

"Let me take a look," he said. Moments later he came back to the window, leaned in, and tapped the fuel gauge. Quite hard.

I let the needle drop down to empty.

"You're out of fuel," he said. "The needle must have got stuck."

"Oh dear," she said. "How silly of me."

"It's easily done," he said. "Hang on and I'll put some petrol in for you. That should see you safely home."

He put in the fuel and completed the paperwork. "Right. That's all sorted. Now, can I offer you a cup of coffee? There's a very nice café just across the road. They do a great black forest gateau."

"No thank you. I'm meeting a friend." Then she stared at him. "Have we met somewhere before?"

He nods. "Last week. When you had a flat tyre."

"Ah yes. I remember, you asked me to go out with you. Well I've already got a boyfriend, so there's no point asking me again." And without another word or backward glance, she puts me in gear, and off we go.

Of course we're late getting to the boyfriend's place. He goes on at her straightaway. "The car keeps letting you down. The car is too old. You need something more modern, more comfortable." The cheek of the man.

If only Patrick was still here. He and Susan were so good together. They were married for twenty two years and still nuts about each other. It was such a shock when he died. I thought that was it, that she'd never look at anyone else, and she didn't, not for three years. Then she met HIM.

Apparently they bumped into each other in Barclays. The first I knew about him was when he decided to have a go at driving me. He jumped in, slammed the door, making me shake, then scraped back the seat to make room for his longer legs.

"Careful," said Susan. "Gertie's not as young as she was."

He didn't take the slightest bit of notice, just revved up my engine until I was breathless, then set off at a furious pace. Susan seldom goes very fast. It's not that she crawls along, getting in everybody's way, she just prefers not to rush everywhere. Doesn't see the point. So when HE put his foot down it was a bit of a shock to my system.

"What's the top speed?" he asked.

"No idea," she replied. "I try to avoid the motorway, so I don't get to go much more than sixty."

"Well today's going to be different," he said.

He was right there. He headed straight for the motorway, and we were off. We zoomed along. Even on the smaller roads, he screeched round all the corners. By the time we got back, I was ready to book myself into the scrap yard. Luckily Susan didn't need me the next day, or I might never have recovered.

We're on our way to see him now. We pull up outside his flat and she honks the horn twice. That's another bad habit he's given her.

"I'll drive," he says, and meek as a kitten, out she gets. I try holding the door shut but he's too strong for me. In he jumps, slams the door, foot down, and we're off before Susan's even managed to do up her seat belt.

"I've got a treat for you," he says. "I've arranged a

test drive for you. Just wait until you try a brand new car. You can have GPS, ABS….."

He lists a whole lot of other things. I haven't a clue what most of them mean, and neither, I suspect, has Susan.

"OK," she says. "Why not, it might be fun. After all, Gertie is getting on a bit."

And I think it's all over.

Luckily for me, the car he's arranged to test drive is another beetle. He's brand new and a bit flash, but luckily for me we speak the same language. While the humans are off talking to the salesman, we exchange a few words.

When they get back from the test drive I can see my new friend has done me proud. The boyfriend has a face as black as thunder.

"You should have let me drive," he said. "We nearly hit that lorry."

"Sorry," she said, "but I just couldn't get on with the gears. I kept finding fourth instead of second."

She slips into my driving seat, then pats me on the dashboard and I know I'm safe. For a while at least.

The atmosphere is stony silence as she drives me back towards his place. There's obviously been more going on than I know about.

It's been a long day but something tells me that this might be the time to try and fix things once and for all between Susan and HIM. So I splutter and cough, and start to get slower and slower.

"What are you doing?" he screeches.

"It's Gertie. She won't go any faster," explains Susan.

"Pull over. Let me drive," he demands crossly. "We haven't got all day."

So he gets in, crunches my gears and pulls away.

I let him get about a hundred yards then as we approach a lay by I make my steering so stiff he has no choice but to pull over.

"I'm not driving this car ever again. It's dangerous," he says as he jumps out.

Susan follows him. "I'd better call the AA," she says.

"Good idea! Maybe they can tow this heap of junk away."

I hold my breath. If they don't send Michael my plan is doomed. When he does turn up, I'm so excited I nearly blow my own horn.

"What's the trouble?" he asks Susan.

"This stupid car," says the boyfriend. "First it goes slow, then it veers off to the left. If it was up to me I'd take it straight to the scrap yard."

"Would you now?" and then he turns to Susan and gives her a butter melting smile. "And what does the lady think?"

And Susan blushes. "Well now, I'm not sure," she says. "I've had this little car for years. She doesn't often let me down."

"No, only all the time," sneers himself. "If you took this lump of metal in for part exchange you'd be lucky to get £50 for it. It's a good job you're well off."

"Actually, "says Michael, "you're wrong there. This lovely little car is worth a whole lot more than £50, aren't you sweetheart?" And he pats my wing ever so tenderly, just like Patrick used to do. If I had arms, I could have hugged him.

The boyfriend looks at me as if he's never seen me before. "How much exactly is it worth?" he asks, unable to keep the little pound signs from flashing on in his eyes, and suddenly Susan sees him for what he is. A shallow gold digger, on the look out for an easier life.

"It doesn't matter how much she's worth. I would never sell Gertie," she says, then she turns to the patrol man and smiles. "Could you take a look at her for me? I'm sure it's nothing serious."

So he looks at the engine, then gets in, turns the ignition key, and wiggles the steering wheel.

"I can't see anything wrong, " he says. "I'd better take a quick look underneath, just in case."

While he's busy, Susan and the boyfriend walk off. I guess they want a bit of privacy. Anyway, it's no surprise that when Michael slides back out from underneath me, Susan is on her own.

"Hop in," he says. "If you could just drive down the lay by a bit, so I can see if the steering's OK now."

I behave perfectly of course.

"What's happened to your boyfriend?" he asks when we come to a stop.

"Oh him," she says. "It's all over. And before you ask, yes, I'd love to go out to dinner with you. Any time you like."

I'm so happy, I feel as if I could fly. I can't help but wonder; maybe there's some truth in this Love Bug thing after all.

Linda Lewis

Linda Lewis (a.k.a. Catherine Howard) is a full-time writer of fiction and non-fiction. She has so many ideas she hardly knows what to do with them. Her short stories are published in UK magazines such as *Take a Break*, as well as in Australia and Scandinavia. She has an agent (Broo Doherty) who is seeking a publisher for her first novel.

Web site – www.lindatorbay.co.uk and www.writespace.co.uk.

Toast and Jam

Great Granny's eyes were a marvel. I don't mean to make fun. I adored her, and still do. But as kids, it was great fun. We'd creep to halfway down the stairs each morning, and watch through the banister rails as she groped her way to the kitchen sink where she'd left her eyeballs soaking overnight in a jam jar. She'd take them out, shake them off, then *pop* them in. Then she'd turn around, and that was the fun part.

Granny's glass eyeballs could be anywhichway in! One up, one down: crossed: both pointing the same way. It was a hoot.

Strangely though, once she'd put her eyes back in her face, it was as if she *could* see. She couldn't of course. But I guess it was psychosomatic stuff, a sort of *optical delusion.*

Great Grandpa was all right too. A tall, gangly, scrawny man with a thin reedy voice … mostly dozing in his deckchair in the shade, or in his armchair beside the fire.

When we kids came to sit with him for a breather between games, he'd come alive and begin to tell us tales. But he was so slow. It was *months* between each word. We got fed up, or slumped down waiting, so the story lost all connection or interest. Half way through it, we'd either have gone to sleep, or gone off to play again, and Grandpa would lapse back into comatose.

It was Granny who told us his stories, sitting around that big old wooden table in the middle of the kitchen each morning … her eyes in all sorts of positions. It was spooky sometimes. It was always toast and jam for breakfast.

"He was a Wizard, you know." She told us. "In his hey day. A powerful one."

We asked, what was his *hey day*?

"When he was young; vital. Vibrant!" she said, punching the air with her balled-up old fist. "He had a *huge* booming voice: could cast spells clear across the valley!"

A big booming voice, we could not imagine. The stories we weren't sure about. But it was Granny's eyes that had us mesmerized. Pointing all over the place! Somehow we *felt* they could see.

It was all one to her, she said. She lived it. She knew it. She was telling us, now. Whether we believed it or not, she couldn't care less: but, *turned that Gwyneth Parr from Pontypridd into a standing stone for lying, he did!*

"That's not really *true,* is it Granny?" asked Mills.

That's not really my Sister's name. I just call her that. Because she's always snitching those sloppy books from the Charity Shop pile Mum puts out after *she's* read them, and *devouring* them by torchlight beneath the bed-clothes when she's supposed to be asleep. I don't know why she liked them. *Boring!* Besides which, Mills is as hard as granite. She'd squash a spider right in front of you without a twitch.

Granny didn't answer. She had become all *far away* and *soft*.

"You're looking at my eyes, aren't you?" she snapped back suddenly.

We sat up, shocked. How did she *know?*

"It was my eyes he fell in love with."

We gaped!

"Oh, I know you wouldn't think that seeing me now: but

then...! I had such *lovely* eyes. Even though I *do* say it myself."

"Grandpa!" I said. "Can I talk to you?"

"Of course, Dear Boy. What is it?"

"Granny's eyes…!"

"Ah! Yes!"

"You *must* have noticed!"

"Indeed, Dear Boy, indeed! "Tis a scary sight!" said Grandpa, shaking his head.

"Can't anything be *done* about them?" I meant, couldn't someone sort of *say something to her*, to make sure she had them in straight, each day. People must wonder whether she was looking at them, or both ways up the road at once. She wasn't bothered herself. But I sort of felt it would be nicer for her, if they were straight.

My question must have started something off in his mind, because Grandpa looked right at me for a full minute without moving. I wondered if he'd died. I was just about to panic and run in for Granny, when he came back to life and said, *it was like this* ...

I realised that he'd been thinking whether or not to tell me, but now, I supposed, had made up his mind.

"It was a windy night, and a frightful storm was brewing. But that was *after* the Sending." For once, Grandpa's voice was strong and unquavering … re-living his memory.

"At the time," he said. "there was a horrible witch called Griselda … Griselda Goomie. Played the bagpipes at dawn. Ye *gods*, what a cacophony! Couldn't stand it! Threatened to turn her into a frog. Granny said don't bother, she already had a tongue bitter enough to freeze horse flies!"

"Was she an old hag?" I asked.

"A bent old ugly crone?" suggested Mills. "With warts!"

"No." said Grandpa. "She was a stunner!" "Truth to tell, she fancied me!" he said. "Imagine!"

We couldn't. Not wrinkly, skeletal old Grandpa.

"Granny called her *Ghastly Goomie*. And it was all because she wanted me, and I didn't want her, that all of it began."

"All of what?"

"Oh, plagues of slimy toads, boils, blasted crops, our well water drying up, that sort of thing. Our beloved Stuff and Nonsense petrified, spread-eagled to a tree. *Nooooo*, Granny was right. Griselda was a *ghastly* witch."

"There are many witches in Wales, Children, and not all *bad,*" said Grandpa. "But Griselda was mad!" "She boasted everywhere that her ancestry was *Druid*, and she was a direct descendant of The Merlin himself."

"And was she?" asked Mills.

"Absolutely not!" stated Grandpa.

"How do you know?" demanded Mills.

"Because *I* am!" said Grandpa.

Mills stared.

"So you *are* a Wizard!" I said, delighted. "We thought it was just Granny's tales."

"*You* did," said Mills. "*I* believed her!"

"Did *not,*" I said.

"*Did!*"

"Children!" boomed Grandpa. We'd never heard his *big booming* voice. And that probably wasn't his *biggest boomiest*. But if it was anything to go by, we were sure it could be heard clear across any valley.

Grandpa leant close. "We are all Wizards and Witches you know. Because we all have *power*. And we can be either *Good,* or *Bad.* It all depends how we wish to

150

use our power. I recommend *Good*."

"Why?" demanded Mills.

"Because of The Law."

"What Law?"

"What goes out, comes back!" said Grandpa. "What you do, comes back to you." "*That* Law!" "Universal Law." "If you're *going* to cast, be very sure it is for Good Intent ... the very best!"

"Oh!" said Mills shortly.

"What about Griselda?" I asked, impatiently.

"Well." Said Grandpa. "It was Christmas Eve, and the Faeries were trimming the Christmas Tree ..."

"*Faeries!*" I snorted.

"In*deed*." He said, giving me a severe look from beneath his beetly old eyebrows. "Faeries trim Christmas Trees with all the Gifts God wants to give Humans."

"Why don't *we* see them, then?" shot in Mills.

"Because you're *too stupid!*" Grandpa shot back.

That shut her up!

"Only those with open hearts and minds can see Faeries." said Grandpa, quite seriously.

I didn't fancy being turned into a frog, so I wiped the smile off my face and nudged Mills. She nudged me back, hard. I scowled at her and rubbed my arm.

"Granny could *always* see them." said Grandpa, becoming all sentimental again.

"Gr*iselda!*" demanded Mills.

"Ah yes! Griselda!" frowned Grandpa. "I never *did* like her. Always suspected her of necromancy." Said Grandpa.

"What's that?" asked Mills.

"Energy Work using dead bodies." Said Grandpa.

"Energy Work?"

"Magic."

"Did you ever use necromancy?"

"No. Never. I've always been vegetarian." Grandpa's eyes slid over to us.

Mills and I stared at him. We didn't move.

Grandpa sighed. "Ah well!" he mumbled, disappointed, and resumed his story.

"It was just before Christmas. A dark evening. Silent and full of snow. Suddenly, there was this *appalling* apparition! Came right through the wall! It was a Sending. A foul thing conjured up by this demented witch. It screeched, *You'll be dead before dawn!* and disappeared."

Mills and I were goggle-eyed!

"I immediately rose to defend myself." said Grandpa, brandishing a fist in the air and half rising from his chair to show us how. "I had no idea it was Griselda. My first thought was to *return* the Sending as a Dove, and so confound the Sender ... being *part* of them, doing so would serve to neutralise their Intent. But my second thought was to follow it to see who the Sender was."

"I should have gone with the first thought." Grandpa deflated, sinking back down into his chair. "If I had," he sighed. "I may have saved Granny's eyes."

Grandpa became maudlin. "Its why I can never tell her which way up her eyes are in!" he mourned.

"*Any*how...!" urged Mills. She had no sentimentality.

"Anyhow," said Grandpa. "I *sent* too. I could anchor and ground within a *milli*second in those days: send, *and* still be actively conscious and aware."

"What does that mean?" I asked.

"I could do more than one thing at once, whilst being in more than one place at once. Consciously! And in control. I was supreme!"

"*Cool!*" I approved, grinning.

"What did you send *as?* An appalling apparition too?" asked Mills.

"Certainly not! I have more sense," said Grandpa. "I sent as a Watcher … a silent, invisible Warrior. I chose Samurai … in case I had to become visible, or defend myself, or both. They are formidable foes, Samurai."

"*And…*" pushed Mills.

"And, I found it was Ghastly Gloomy Griselda Goomie!"

"And you *blasted* her on the spot!" said Mills. "*Lopped off her head!*"

"I did not!"

Mills' face fell.

"I was a Watcher! I watched!" said Grandpa.

"What did you see?" I asked.

"More than you'll ever know!"

"Why?"

"Because I shan't tell you!" snapped Grandpa. He could be quite peevish at times.

We groaned, and subsided.

"I saw Griselda amassing an army," said Grandpa. "She was almost finished, which was *why* the Sending. Luckily for me, she had no idea it had gone out. She was so intent at her evil concoctions, that she was unaware one of her angry thought-forms had escaped her. Which is precisely what I meant by being consciously aware *and* active, simultaneously. Its an *Art*, you know." His head drooped. "But I was powerful then" he said, sadly, as if he had lost something.

"*So…!*" prompted Mills.

"So shocked was I, that I pulled myself back in! *Not* a very *skilled* thing to do!" lamented Grandpa.

"*But…!*" urged Mills.

"But, I'm ashamed to say, that in those few moments, Griselda finished her unwholesome business, became aware of *my* Sending, and began her attack."

"Then arose that great storm. Thunder, lightening, snow, hail, sleet, rain, wind … *everything!* The wind screeched and howled. All our windows and doors opened and shut and banged and slammed. Glass shattered. Bushes and branches broke off and hurled themselves at us." Grandpa shivered.

"What did you do?" I asked.

"I *should* have commanded them to be still, then gone out to meet the enemy. I love the world and have no fear of its power. Because it knows this, it would never harm me. But in my panic, I forgot that. Instead, I let it rant and rave and beat at us. Granny was transfixed to the sitting room wall by a small tornado!"

Mills and I imagined it.

"And suddenly there was this mighty army at my door, brandishing weapons and wailing like hordes of bloodcurdling banshees," Said Grandpa. "The attack went on all night. Then just before dawn, Griselda arrived to do her grizzly work."

"She was *breath-taking!*" remembered Grandpa. "Topped the house by *yards!*" "Her face was all lit up … a fearsome, phosphorescent green colour. Her eyes glowed red hell-fire and shot shards of psychic energy at us, designed to maim, to disfigure, to kill. She'd have us twisted tormented wretches, or corpsed. *Dead before dawn!*"

We waited open-mouthed.

"I dodged about: here, there, all over the place. She'd caught me off guard, and I'm embarrassed to say that I fled for the cupboard under the stairs." Said Grandpa.

Mills was disgusted. You could see her thinking, *wimp!* She had no time for battered Princes. Mills wanted Grandpa to have battled for Granny, and won!

"But before I could get there, Granny screamed, *Huw! Do something!*"

"What did you do?" I asked.

"Hid behind the sofa."

"*What!*" shouted Mills, *utterly* gone off Grandpa! *Some* Wizard!

"I know." Said Grandpa, hanging his head. "I'm ashamed to *say*. But then something came to my aid."

"What?"

"Courage!"

"I collected my wits, and focussed my energy." Grandpa recalled. "Powerful once again, I stood up. By this time we were surrounded by fire. There was no way out. And it was coming closer. Soon, we'd burn."

"Fiery Imps came in through all the openings. Lightening bolts rained down on our roof. My beloved apple tree was blasted, blossom to bole. Ghoulish creatures attacking us. The power was *awesome* that night."

"Then Griselda turned her attention to Granny." Said Grandpa. "She drew her bodily up the chimney by the sheer force of her amazing will power. I ran outside, and there was Granny, suspended in mid air above the house!"

Mills and I were speechless. Grandpa continued.

"Buffeted and beaten by weather and supernatural energy, poor Granny hung there in the night sky looking for all the world like some horrible blazing star!" "It was a terrible sight!"

"If Griselda let go, Granny would crash to her death … something that would crush me. And Griselda knew it. She was out to get her own back! *Ghastly* woman!" Grandpa shook his head, remembering.

"Then Griselda saw me, and began firing lightening bolts … chased me round and round the house with them, laughing insanely with each shot."

"*Grand*pa!" exclaimed Mills. She was all bent out of shape with him.

"I know!" agreed Grandpa, humiliated with himself. "And worse!" he said.

Mills' face darkened.

"While she chased me, Griselda took her eyes of Granny for an instant, and Granny put *her* eyes on Griselda! She was *so* angry, her eyes shot Fire, and then came the blinding battle between them."

"But it gave *me* a chance. I drew up my power. Then dealt with the horrible hordes."

"How?" asked Mills.

"Easy!" said Grandpa. "One fights dark with Light. Against Light, dark has no power. Light is Truth. Dark is *without* Truth. So I attacked them with a Sword of Light! Cut, stabbed, beheaded, slashed them to shreds, *chop, chop, chop!*" Grandpa *chopped* and *slashed* his hands about in the air around him.

"None can stand against the Light!" he declared grandly.

"Finally, I shouted Words of Power!" said Grandpa, eyes gleaming with remembrance.

"Then I turned my attention to the Elements. I fought Fire with Fire. I summoned Salamander … *Salamander: Hear me!*" I commanded. "*I honour you in all your terrible might, and do command you, by the power of my love for you, to stop your terrible work: Earth, Wind and Water, I do hereby command you also, to refrain and desist. You have been created by hate, and against my will! I call you now by name to be at Peace!*"

Grandpa stood. His hand lifted up in the air. Like a Policeman demanding *STOP!*

"I called each by their true Names, known only to the Initiated: but I cannot tell you them, for you are not an Initiate. And hearing their real names called, they knew my will to be true and Griselda's false, and in that moment, all their frightening force turned whence it had come, and wreaked havoc upon that immoral creature Griselda Goomie!"

"You see, Children," said Grandpa. "Magic is only knowing your Power; but you must never use it for dark intent." He said, eyeing us intently.

"What happened to her?"

"She was all shrivelled up into a twisted heap of blithering idiocy."

"Cripes!"

"Like I told you, Children … *never flout the Law!*

"And Granny?" asked Mills.

"Granny took the full force of it all." sighed Grandpa. "She sacrificed her eyes, fighting Griselda … the *wicked witch!* The fire, the lightening, the *pure energy expended,* burned her poor eyes out." Said Grandpa.

Mills and I sat, stunned.

"She did it for love, you know." Mourned Grandpa. "And I've never been able to *say* anything about it since. I feel so *guilty!* It was *all* my fault!

"*I* should say so!" retorted Mills, pouting.

Grandpa nodded. "I blamed myself. Felt so *bad* about my *weakness!* Sank down into depression. You see people do that all the time … take the blame, be overcome with remorse and self-pity, and then it's all over for them: they *give away their power. Ugly* sight!" "But that's what *I* did too!"

"Can't *anything* be done for Granny?" I asked softly, ending where I'd begun.

We visited *The Grands*, Summer and Winter. This was Winter … Christmas. And as soon as Grandpa had said it,

157

an unspoken pact passed between Mills and myself to sit up all night and see for ourselves the Faeries trim the Christmas Tree. But although we tried hard, we fell asleep. How Granny didn't trip over us coming downstairs the next morning, was a miracle. How did she *know* we were there?

She went through the usual morning pantomime of putting in her glass eyes, then turned around sharply and said, *Grandpa's gone!* One of her eyes was pointing up and out, and the other was inspecting the inside edge of her nose, but she *looked* directly at us where we sat on the stairs still waiting for the Faeries. How did she *do* it?

"Where?" exclaimed Mills.

"Don't know." Said Granny. "Just gone!" Then her face broke out into a huge grin and she said, "Get any good gifts, then?"

Mills and I looked at each other. She knew!

"We waited up to see the Faeries." I confessed.

Mills dug me in the ribs and glowered.

"You're such a *tell*-tale!" she complained.

"She already knows!" I hissed at her.

"Well, you needn't have bothered." Granny said, making toast and jam.

"Why not?" asked Mills.

"They've already been and gone!" she chortled.

I felt really let down. I stuck my tongue out at Mills.

We waited all morning for Grandpa to return. Granny didn't say another word about him. She didn't seem bothered at all. So we decided we shouldn't be bothered either, and at noon, Mills and I trundled off to Farmer Jenk's place across the fields, on a special errand we had agreed upon earlier. Mrs Jenks made great homemade wines … Beetroot, Parsnip, Elderflower … *loads* of different ones. The Grands loved them. We settled terms with them, and stowed away our package as best we could, then went back indoors. By teatime there was still no sign of Grandpa.

There were no stories that day. It just passed as most normal days do. Toast and jam, collected firewood, had supper, then went to bed early … pretending we were tired. Granny nodded, and kept on knitting beside the fire.

As quietly as we could, we wrapped up our Christmas present for The Grands, but it wasn't easy.

And then it was Christmas morning.

We rushed down early, and put our parcel beneath the tree. And there were piles of other presents! Mills and I grinned at one another.

Granny came down and made us toast and jam, but there was still no sign of Grandpa. None of us mentioned it.

Then suddenly Grandpa appeared. He wasn't there, and then he was! I *know* he came through the wall!

We gaped at him, gaped at each other, then squeaked, "Where have you *been!*"

Of course, we hoped he'd been to get us some surprise presents. And he had … for Granny.

"I had a little *Universal* work to do." He said, grinning from ear to ear, and as powerful as any Wizard! "Had to have a word with the Universal Council. Had an old wrong to put right. Made my apologies and was granted special dispensation as reward, because it was a Gift of Love. Look!" he said, and we turned to look at Granny.

She was sitting at that big old wooden kitchen table, crying her eyes out. *Her* eyes! She'd been given them back, somehow. It was magic!

"*How!*" I asked, incredulously.

"By the Grace of God!" said Grandpa.

And Granny had been right … she had *lovely* eyes … soft and grey and *very* deep and full of love.

Mills and I were so impressed and happy and delighted, that we gave The Grands their present right away. Which was probably a good idea. If we'd left it much longer, they'd probably have suffocated. Two kittens … Stuff & Nonsense the Seconds, we said.

We had been wondering what to get The Grands for Christmas, and after we'd heard about their *first* two Stuff and Nonsenses, these seemed to be just the job … two little black balls of fluff from Farmer Jenks.

"*Ooooooohh!* cried Granny. "*Just* what I wanted! *All* my Christmas Gifts come together in one go!"

When it came time for us to leave that winter, I didn't want to go. I had to stay to help the two kittens, I said.

"They're quite capable of *helping* themselves." Granny grinned. "Cats are quite independent."

"*You* need help, now you've got *eyes*." I said.

"I could have done with help *before* I got eyes." Granny smiled.

I even contemplated having some horrible spotty sickness … being at death's door … that kind of thing. But finally Granny persuaded me that there was always *next* holidays. And may*be*, Faeries too, she said, and winked at me!

Oscar Peebles

"I live on the South Coast where I write Fantastical and Metaphysical stories conjured up by the wind and waves, for all reading ages. I use pseudonyms, as I think the story is the star, not the author. My lovely Mum introduced me to the world of books and my Pa to the absurd and faintly wicked. I can be found at joblurb@googlemail.com" says Oscar.

The Blue List

1 – Give Up smoking
2 – Stop eating so much junk food
3 – Help an old lady with her shopping
4 – Drink less beer
5 – Spend less time watching TV
6 – Meet a nice girl and go steady.

It was 7.30 on New Years Eve. I'd just finished a frozen pizza. One of the soaps was on TV, I wasn't sure which one.

I turned the piece of bright blue paper over in my hand. It was last years' resolutions made in an after midnight haze. Most of them made sense, but help an old lady with her shopping? I had no idea where that one came from.

I had achieved none of them. I managed without a cigarette for exactly one hour. A year on and I was still eating the same diet of pizzas, burgers and take aways, still a slave to the one eyed God, as I called the TV.

I found the list as I rummaged in a drawer looking for a piece of paper on which to scribble this year's resolutions. All at once, there didn't seem to be much point.

I was nearly thirty. Still on my own, living in an easy to care for flat, conveniently situated ten minutes from work and five minutes from a fish and chip shop. Worst of all, I still had no steady girl in my life.

Most of my friends were married, or much younger than I was. One or two were divorced and already embarking on their next serious relationship. The sudden realisation came to me – I was in a rut. Self pity was about to take hold when the telephone rang.

"Hi Nick, it's Dean. We're all going to the Black Horse tonight. It's got a bar extension till 2 a.m. Better than the Royal Oak, eh?" I muttered something and he went on. "Are you going?"

I found myself saying no, "I'm not in the mood. I'll catch up with everyone later."

As I put down the phone, a man on the local news was rabbitting on about the New Year, saying it was a time of opportunity, a time to change, to start over. I looked at my long forgotten list and was filled with a determination to do better this year. I decided to start by tackling one of last year's resolutions before I thought about making any new ones.

I searched everywhere for a pin, but all I could find was a fork. I spread the blue paper on the table, smoothed out the creases, then closed my eyes, and stabbed the list with the fork. It landed on Number 2 – eat less junk food.

I sighed and went to the fridge. A few cans of beer, some lemonade, a pint of milk, a pack of Flora, some Dairylea and half a loaf of white sliced bread.

The kitchen cupboards revealed eleven tins of baked beans, a dozen packets of pot noodle, a packet of spaghetti a year past its sell by date, three tins of soup, some cream crackers (stale), a jar of Branston, two opened jars of pickled onions (great with fish and chips), six jars of peanut butter (two smooth and four crunchy), and an almost empty jar of marmalade.

There wasn't a piece of fruit, or a vegetable, to be seen, unless you counted the baked beans.

It was early. I could go to the supermarket, and still get to the pub at a reasonable hour.

I grabbed my coat and set off. If I bought loads of proper food and filled up the fridge with fresh vegetables,

I could start the New Year happy. If it was there, I'd have to eat it. Wasting food wasn't in my nature.

It was strangely quiet at Tescos, presumably people had already stocked up for the siege.

Instead of taking my usual sharp right turn and heading toward the frozen pizzas, I went straight ahead into the uncharted waters of the fresh fruit and vegetable aisles. I had no idea what I was going to buy.

It wasn't that I didn't know how to cook: when I lived at home, Mum insisted I took my turn in the kitchen along with my sisters, it's just that everything looked 'difficult.' Why bother to peel a potato when you can buy chips, or slice up carrots when you can pop a frozen pizza in the oven, or better still, microwave a curry?

A small voice behind me broke my train of thought. "Excuse me, young man, could you fetch me down a bag of satsumas? I can't quite reach."

"Of course," I said as I smiled down from my six feet two at the old lady who'd appeared, silently, at my side.

"Thank you, young man," she said, as she disappeared down the aisle. I thought no more of it until I reached the checkouts. Just in front of me was the same little old lady. I hoped she had a car. Her bulging bags looked awkward and rather heavy. Resolution number four popped into my head, but I'd helped her already by getting a bag down off the top shelf.

I unloaded my purchases on to the conveyor belt. I'd decided not to go mad, just buy a few things to give this new way of eating a chance – some jacket potatoes (easily microwaved), a packet of sausages, some carrots, two large onions, two pints of milk, a loaf, and three bananas.

As I stepped outside into the already chill night air, I almost bumped into the old woman. She was standing under the shelter looking to left and right. "Are you OK?" I asked her.

"My granddaughter's meant to be picking me up. Only she's not here."

It wasn't my problem, the granddaughter would be sure to turn up soon, but then that blue list popped into my head. "Where do you live?"

She gave me an address, not five minutes from my own flat.

"If you like, I could give you a lift."

"I'm not sure. Fiona might spend ages looking for me."

"Has she got a mobile?"

"Yes."

"You can call her – say you're on your way home. She can meet you there."

The old woman peered at my bright yellow phone. "I've never used one of those. Can you do it for me?"

There was no reply, so I left a message, telling a woman I didn't know that I was giving her Gran a lift home. "I left a message. Is that OK?"

She said, yes it was, so I helped her into the car, put her bags in the boot, and took her home. As I drove she hardly stopped talking. I found out her name – Mrs Adams, how old she was – 85, loads about her granddaughter – Fiona, twenty six, recently divorced, no children, librarian, and that they were spending the evening together, sharing a meal and some red wine.

She was still chatting as a key turned in the lock.

A young woman walked in.

"Hello Fiona. This is Nick . He gave me a lift, and helped me with my shopping."

"I left a message on your phone," I said, as I put the last tin away and turned to leave.

"I didn't have my phone with me," she said giving her Gran a glare.

"But she said…."

Before I could finish the sentence, the girl turned to the old lady. "You've been up to your tricks again, haven't you?"

"Maybe," she replied with a grin.

"I'd best be off then," I said not wanting to get involved in a row.

"Don't go," said Mrs Adams. "It's New Year's Eve. We could use some extra company."

"Now stop that, Gran. I expect Nick has people waiting for him."

As she spoke, I thought of Barry and Jim, Terry and Mike. They'd be well into party mode by now. "I'm meant to be meeting my mates, down the pub," I said.

"You don't sound keen. Do you HAVE to go?" asked Mrs Adams.

"No, I don't have to," I agreed.

Fiona took her Gran's hand and squeezed it between hers. "Let him go to his friends. He doesn't want to spend New Year's Eve with an old woman and a bookworm."

I started to say something, but Fiona was still talking.

"This is the fourth time you've gone to the supermarket and come back with a strange man. I've told you so many times before, I don't need your help finding a date, besides, it could be dangerous."

Mrs Adams raised her hands in mock surrender. "I'm sorry dear, but I just can't help myself. A lovely young girl like you shouldn't be spending her time all alone."

"I'm not alone, Gran, I've got you."

"Goodbye then," I managed to say at last.

The girl turned to me and sighed. "Look, you can stay if you like. I don't mind. We've got way too much food as usual." She glared at Mrs Adams, but the warmth was there to see.

I didn't protest again. To be honest, the appeal of the Black Horse had faded the moment I saw Fiona.

She reminded me of a pixie. She looked small, delicate, although as she stood close to me I could see she was easily five feet six, maybe more. Her grey eyes danced with life and mischief. I got the feeling that being round her could be fun.

I was right, it was the best New Year's Eve I ever had.

The food was delicious.

We played games I'd only ever heard of before – Cluedo and Pictionary. I was hopeless, but it didn't seem to matter. My sides ached from laughing so much.

As we played and talked, I watched the two of them together, sixty years apart in age, but so close in other ways. Their love for each other shone like a star, so warm it even reached my cold heart. Fiona opened a bottle of Rioja and as the chimes of Big Ben rang through the house, we drank a toast to the New Year. 2008 was no more.

"Aren't you going to share a New Year kiss?" demanded Mrs Adams. "It's traditional."

Fiona raised her eyebrows. "Best do what she says, or I'll never hear the last of it," she laughed.

As I bent my head to kiss her, she slipped an arm round my waist and pulled me closer. I wanted that kiss to last forever, but it was over in a moment.

As we drew apart, Mrs Adams prodded me in the back. "Now be off with you. It's time I got to my bed."

I reached into my pocket for my diary. "Give me your number and I'll call you, that's if you'd like me to."

"It's 263116," said Mrs Adams.

Fiona laughed out loud. "Gran! I do know my own number. What if I didn't want Nick to call me?"

But I could tell by the way that she said it, that she DID want me to.

As I got into the car and started the engine, a thin veil of frost was already forming. The two of them were still laughing and chatting as I pulled away.

It was a strange feeling, arriving home with a clear head. The night was so still. I felt oddly contented as I unloaded my shopping. Inside the flat, the blue list was on the table where I'd left it. As I read it, I smiled.

I was sober. I hadn't had a cigarette for six hours (a record for me when awake). The fridge contained at least some good, wholesome food. I'd helped an old lady with her shopping. The TV was off, and best of all, I'd met the nicest girl in Devon, who seemed to like me as much as I liked her.

As I drifted off to sleep, I decided not to make any new resolutions. Last year's would do just fine. After all, I only had one more to tackle, and that was half done already.

Linda Lewis

Linda Lewis (a.k.a. Catherine Howard) is a full-time writer of fiction and non-fiction. She has so many ideas she hardly knows what to do with them. Her short stories are published in UK magazines such as *Take a Break*, as well as in Australia and Scandinavia. She has an agent (Broo Doherty) who is seeking a publisher for her first novel.

Web site – www.lindatorbay.co.uk and www.writespace.co.uk.

Murder in the Air

Belinda smoothed down her airhostess uniform, served dinner to the first class passengers, administered poison to the man in the front row, switched off the cabin lights and entered the galley. She washed her hands twice, scrubbing between the fingers and under the fingernails. With a disposable tissue, she wiped a small sachet (in case the porous paper managed to retain fingerprints), and threw it into the trash bin in the galley. Everything was going according to plan.

Then she hesitated. Slowly, ever so slowly, she bent down to retrieve the sachet. Yes. It made a lot more sense to change the plan and dispose of the sachet in the passengers' WC. Why hadn't she realised it before?

"Belinda, are you all right?"

Belinda flinched, but she kept her on-the-job smile on as she turned to face one of the other girls. "Sure, Cathy. Why do you ask?"

"You look flushed, darling. Does it have anything to do with that passenger you are seeing? You know, the one who travels first class with us from Bangkok every week?"

"I'm not seeing anybody," Belinda could feel the heat in her cheeks. "I'm engaged, remember?" She held up her hand so that Cathy could look at her ring. If you didn't know, you might think the diamond was real. "Whatever made you think -"

"Don't worry, Bel. I won't tell a soul."

"Won't tell what?"

"That I saw the two of you together yesterday. In the centre of the Patpong red light district? Whispering like a pair of lovers -"

"Someone's calling you," interrupted Belinda. She

felt dizzy. Damn Cathy all the way to Hell! What was she doing in that part of town, anyway? There was nothing but sleaze in Patpong: no jewellery shops, no interesting temples.

Think, Belinda, think. Cathy might promise not to tell now, but what will she say to the police tomorrow when the passenger in the front row is found dead in his seat?

*   *   *

It was purely by accident that Belinda became an airhostess. At school, she hadn't thought further than the next party. When someone asked what she wanted to be when she grew up, Belinda would say the first thing that came to mind. "A doctor," she had said on her tenth birthday. "A secretary," she announced five years later. "An airhostess," she said when she turned eighteen. By then, she knew better than to expect the job to be a string of exciting trips to foreign countries. But it didn't matter one bit, because she wasn't serious about becoming an airhostess anyway.

Not until Jerry twisted his lips into a crooked grin and fired, "An airhostess? Fancy that. I thought they only employed *beautiful* girls."

Jerry. Belinda smiled. Jerry. To impress him, she had applied for an airhostess position with a major airline, sailed through the interview, which involved being measured and weighed, and visited Jerry wearing a triumphant smile and a pretty sapphire uniform.

"I hope you realise you'll simply be a glamorized waitress," he'd said, his fingers stroking the fabric of her airhostess skirt. "Serving dinner, cleaning up and disposing of nausea-bags filled with sick. Single male passengers will hit on you and turn nasty if you don't play along.

You will earn next to nothing and there won't be any tips. And in no time at all, you'll be twenty-five and your career will be over. There will be others, years younger than you, queuing up for your job. Whatever will you do then?"

Belinda never let herself forget that question.

* * *

The aeroplane toilet for the first-class crowd was almost as tiny as the cattle class cubicle, but the disposable towels were thicker, there were cold cream jars and aftershave lotions on the shelf, and the soap smelled of almond. Almond... Belinda pursed her lips and crumpled up the paper sachet. Fingerprints? She smoothed out the wrinkles with a tissue and wiped vigorously.

Then she froze. DNA tests! How could she have not thought of it before?

Was she brave enough to dispose of the sachet by eating it, knowing what it had contained? Belinda shivered. Her knowledge of poisons and lethal doses was sound, thanks to hours of research in anonymous Internet Cafes, and yet she couldn't bring herself to swallowing the sachet that had contained the deadly powder.

She let hot water run over the sachet. The paper began to disintegrate. Belinda rubbed it between her palms. When the paper pulped, she threw it in the bin. If anybody questioned her DNA on it, why, what's more natural for an airhostess than to pick up a piece of rubbish and throw it out?

Satisfied at last, she pushed the hatch of the disposal bin. All done. Now she could catch some sleep.

Slipping out of the toilet cubicle, she suddenly became aware of a shadow on the wall. With a sense of foreboding, she watched Cathy's shoulders disappear down the stairs to the main cabin. What was Cathy doing upstairs, in the first class part of the plane, when business class was her usual area?

I have to do something about Cathy, Belinda thought.

* * *

She'd been planning it for months. Reading about arsenic and strychnine, learning that even ordinary aspirin can be poisonous, albeit not lethally so. But knowing all the time that it would be cyanide. Jerry used it to kill butterflies for his collection. Ether would have achieved the same, but Jerry insisted on cyanide. It made him feel important, "For goodness' sake, whatever you do, don't open the cupboard in my study," he would warn his guests. He'd pause, then grin: "I store my cyanide there!"

So cyanide it would be. A present for Jerry, from the prettiest butterfly in his collection.

* * *

Belinda was about to sit down in her Spartan airhostess chair when the service light flickered. She sighed. Some people. They'd pay a fortune for the first class ticket, the equivalent of her own quarterly earnings (the *regular* ones, that is), but instead of enjoying the comfort, they would toss and turn all night, requesting champagne, a snack, another magazine....

Soon, Belinda promised herself, soon she would be just like them. Thanks to the passenger in the front row by the window. She avoided looking in that direction.

"Ms Rogers?" she whispered, bending over the plump elderly woman and switching off the service light. That was part of the job, knowing the rich passengers by name and remembering which ones of the regulars take lemon in their tea and who prefers milk. "How can I help you, ma'am?"

171

Soon, she would have enough money to buy first class tickets and sprawl in one of the deep armchairs and let somebody else remember how many sugars she took in her tea. But would she want to travel? Or would she simply go shopping in designer stores by day, and dance with Jerry in luxurious hotels at night?

"Another brandy to help you sleep, ma'am? Oh, something sweeter? Amaretto... of course, Ms Rogers, right away."

Amaretto. The smell of almonds invaded Belinda's nostrils again as she poured the amber liquid. The passenger in the front row had had a cold. How fortunate. He hadn't smelled a thing.

*   *   *

Cyanide prevents the body's red blood cells from absorbing oxygen, Belinda recalled, as she put away the bottle of Amaretto, *causing immediate unconsciousness, convulsions and death.*

That could have presented a problem. Had Mr Fisher began gasping for breath, he could have alerted the other passengers. Fortunately, Mr Fisher had been in the habit of taking sleeping pills. "I can't sleep in anything that moves, my dear," he always told her as he requested tea after his three-course first class dinner. He would wash down his caviar and two blue capsules with a full cup of disgustingly weak milky brew.

Last night, of course, his tea emitted a faint aroma of almond. Thoughtfully, Belinda had included an almond biscotti to go with his tea, to account for the smell. Mr Fisher had accepted it with a confident "thank you," and he curled his short fat fingers around her long slim ones for a second.

Even now, Belinda shook off the feeling of distaste

172

as she remembered the touch of his rubbery skin on hers.

"Your Amaretto, Ms Rogers. I hope you enjoy it. Please let me know if there is anything else you might need to make your journey more comfortable."

"Thank you, love. You're a good kid."

Guilt hit Belinda right in the hollow of her stomach. I'm not a good kid, she thought. I did what I did because I want a break, a chance to set myself up in life, a retirement fund for when crow's feet make me unfit to do this job. I know what I want, and I went for it.

And the cost? The life of another human being, a despicable human being, to be sure, but a human being nonetheless.

His life for mine, she thought.

It made her feel even worse.

*   *   *

Pouring cyanide into a sachet in Jerry's bathroom had been easy, just one firm flick of a wrist. She even remembered to wipe the jar and replace it in the cupboard exactly as she had found it.

"Happy birthday, Belinda," Jerry had said when she returned to the lounge. There was a loud pop and the murmur of sparkling wine on glass. "Thought I'd forgotten your twenty-fourth, didn't you?"

"Oh, Jerry!" She raised her glass, tasted the cheap bubbles. Suddenly, she froze as she noticed something at the bottom of the glass, something round and golden and very glittery.

"I can't ask you to marry me, girl," Jerry smiled his sorrowful lopsided smile. "I didn't even have money for a real diamond. But I was hoping you'd say yes anyway, and then, perhaps, one day -"

Sooner than you imagine, Belinda had thought, patting the sachet full of cyanide hidden safely in her pocket.

*   *   *

The plane entered an air pocket and jolted. Belinda opened her eyes and consulted her watch. Almost time to prepare breakfast. She rubbed her eyes. Then she remembered.

The guilt was even worse the morning after. It took all of Belinda's strength to perform her morning routine.

"Good morning Ms Rogers. Did you manage to get any sleep in the end? What would you like for breakfast? Certainly, ma'am. Good morning, Dr Lake. Your usual? Coming right up. The weather is going to be lovely, the captain says. Good morning, Mr Fisher. Mr Fisher?"

Assuming a concerned expression, Belinda shook the stiff shoulder. She had planned to faint and let somebody else deal with Mr Fisher's untimely demise. But that might have caused panic among the passengers. Years of professional behaviour took over against her will.

"Certainly, sir," she smiled at the dead man. "I'll wake you just as soon as we land in Johannesburg. Let me just take that pillow from you. I know they make your neck stiff."

She stowed away the pillow, turned around and headed for the cockpit.

It was only with the cockpit door firmly shut behind her, that she said: "Captain, we have a problem."

And then she closed her eyes and slid carefully to the floor. The cockpit was not big enough to lie down in, but she made the best of the space available.

I wonder what Mr Fisher was doing with a pillow, she thought as she waited for somebody else to deal with the situation.

*   *   *

"It's probably all my fault," Belinda sobbed in the airport

rest room. She was glad that she could hide her face on Cathy's shoulder, because that meant that she didn't have to bother with her mimicry. "He looked a bit off when I saw him last night, but I didn't think anything of it. Perhaps he was feeling unwell? I should have asked him whether he was up to flying. I should have checked up on him after lights out."

"Don't upset yourself, Bel. You just did your job. You did everything you were supposed to do."

And then some, Belinda thought.

"Oh Cathy, the police will never believe I'm innocent! Not when they find out that I knew him! Not when they find out I was the one who served him his meal last night."

"I won't tell the police about your being friendly with him, darling. I promise. But I hope you can help me in return?"

Belinda raised her eyebrows in a silent question.

"It's just that, you see, I'm so terribly broke at the moment. It's temporary, of course, and I'll pay you back just as soon as my luck changes at the roulette table, but in the meantime, could you lend me a few grand?"

*   *   *

The policeman seemed friendly enough, polite in that slightly patronising and slightly chauvinist manner that belonged to the older generation of Afrikaner men. He introduced himself as Detective van Rooyen.

"Just tell me in your own words what happened, Miss," he said.

Belinda did, starting at helping Mr Fisher to his seat and ending with finding him dead. She omitted a few crucial details.

"So you were the only person serving him last night?

175

The champagne and macadamia nuts on boarding the aircraft, the Perrier, the dinner with the wine, the tea?"

"Yes." Belinda's left thumb found her cheap engagement ring and twisted it round and round on her finger. "Unless he ate something in the VIP lounge, before boarding."

Did that come across too eager to lay the blame elsewhere? The detective looked at her, without saying a word, his face devoid of expression. He simply waited for her to continue. Belinda fought the urge to fill the silence with unnecessary words, words that might incriminate her.

Her patience was eventually rewarded.

"Did you know Mr Fisher well, Miss?" asked Detective van Rooyen.

Belinda had prepared for the question. "He was a regular passenger. He travelled on that Friday flight from Bangkok several times a month. I knew him as well as I do any regular first class passenger."

"But how well did you know him outside of the aeroplane?"

Belinda felt her hands go clammy. "What do you mean?"

The detective's expression was still blank. "We have reason to believe you knew Mr Fisher in your private capacity."

Belinda took a tiny handkerchief out of her jacket's pocket and pressed it to her lips. Hard. The pain did the trick. Her eyes started to sting. She continued the pressure on the tender spot until a large tear rolled down her cheek. She knew she looked pretty and vulnerable.

"I'm sorry," she whispered, not bothering to wipe away the tear. "This is all so very difficult."

The detective nodded encouragingly.

"We're not supposed to get friendly with the customers of our airline," Belinda began. "I could lose my job over this."

That was a clever trick, she thought, to pretend to worry about the job at this point.

Van Rooyen hastened to promise discretion if what she'd said had nothing to do with the case. That gave Belinda a chance to fabricate her new lie.

"It's only that, you see, Mr Fisher felt bored in Bangkok. On a few occasions, he asked me to accompany him on sightseeing tours. We went to see the Emerald Buddha and explored the city together."

"So you knew him pretty well then?"

"Not really. He didn't say much during those trips. We'd meet up and stroll together or share a taxi if the weather was too hot. I talked mostly about my fiancé," Belinda glanced pointedly at her engagement ring, "and Mr Fisher listened."

"That's not quite how I have it," said van Rooyen.

Belinda pulled a shocked face. "Sometimes people invent gossip where there is none," she murmured.

"And did you get, ahem, financially rewarded for these sightseeing trips?"

Belinda didn't have to act the flush that flooded her cheeks.

"I most certainly did not!"

At the end of the interview the standard question came. Had she noticed anything unusual, a small detail that had been off, even if it seemed totally irrelevant to the investigation…

Belinda wondered whether it was safe to mention how tired Mr Fisher had acted.

*   *   *

When they'd met in Patpong that Wednesday, Mr Fisher

had given her the dealer's address.

"I'm too busy to deliver the goods myself this time, Doll," he'd said. He always called her Doll, and he always put his hand on her thigh whenever the opportunity presented itself, his fat fingers crawling under her short skirt. He said "too busy", but his grey face and lacklustre eyes looked drained. "Soon I might have to stop this particular enterprise altogether."

With the address of the dealer, Mr Fisher had given her a larger than usual consignment. That's when Belinda had known she had to put her plan into action on the very next flight.

*   *   *

"Miss," said Detective van Rooyen. "Did you notice anything unusual -"

"No, I'm sorry," replied Belinda. "Nothing that I can think of."

She pocketed the business card with Detective van Rooyen's contact details and promised to be in touch should she remember anything.

*   *   *

"A nice rack," said van Rooyen. "Much better than the previous one."

"And did you see those cheeks?" his partner made fondling gestures in the air. "I'd love to book her just to have an opportunity to help her sweet bottom up into the van. Hey, can we do that? She was the last person to see the dead man alive. And she served him his food."

"Hold your horses. We don't know the M.O. yet."

"Still. I would book her. Or at least follow her."

"You mean, have her followed," grinned van Rooyen.

"Nah. Why give anybody else the pleasure?"

Belinda waited a whole week before she felt secure enough to recover the parcel she had hidden in the airport's crew rest room the day after the murder. She went into one of the booths and opened the water reservoir. She breathed a sigh of relief. It was still there, taped to the underside of the lid, a sealed plastic bag containing a more than a kilogram of the highest quality cocaine.

It had belonged to Mr Fisher. Like many before it.

But this time Belinda would do more than carry it through customs taped to her bare skin under her pretty uniform. This time, she would sell it herself and pocket the full amount.

And then what, Belinda mused. Would she become Jerry's wife, the crown of his butterfly collection? Odd, the more she thought about the marriage, the less she desired it.

And the more she blamed Jerry for what she had done.

If only he hadn't mocked her into becoming an airhostess. If only he were able to make more money. If only he didn't keep cyanide in his cupboard....

*   *   *

"We finally have the autopsy results," said Detective van Rooyen to his partner.

"What took them so long?"

"Talcum powder."

"Huh?"

Van Rooyen enjoyed the effect of his news. "Talcum powder, you know, like what ladies put between their boobies? They found a substantial quality in his stomach, injested around the time he'd had his dinner on the plane."

"Is talcum powder poisonous?"

179

"Nope. The victim died of asphyxiation. The doctor's best guess is, smothered with a blanket or a pillow. But it took them a while to figure out what the powder in his stomach was."

"So why did he eat talcum powder? Licked it off his girlfriend, you think?"

"You are sick, you know that, Smith?"

"Yeah."

*   *   *

The poshest suburb of Johannesburg was all security fences and garden walls taller than the houses they enclosed. There were no street signs and it took Belinda many dead ends in her rented car to realise that the street names were painted on the kerbs.

Eventually she reached the correct house and parked across the wide lane, three gardens down. She'd been warned not to walk anywhere by herself, that the city was not safe, but the warning seemed ridiculous in this tranquil residential area.

She had approached the wrought-iron gate, but before she could ring the bell, the front door of the drug mansion swung open.

A familiar silhouette emerged from the house. Belinda had just enough time to duck behind the purple tangles of a bougainvillea tree.

From the safety of her hiding place, Belinda watched Cathy and the drug dealer walk to the gate. He didn't look like a drug dealer at all, more like a successful business-man or a politician. He and Cathy shook hands. Cathy's smile was as wide as her jaw.

My-my, thought Belinda. Mr Fisher's enterprise was larger than I imagined.

Then another thought struck her: if Cathy had also

been Mr Fisher's carrier, she would have had just as good a motive for killing him.

Belinda thought back to the night of the murder. Fact one: Cathy had been upstairs in the first class cabin where she had no reason to be. Fact two: the pillow on the dead man's armchair even though he never used them. Fact three: Cathy needed money.

Belinda swallowed hard. Fact four, she reminded herself: it was she, not Cathy, who laced Mr Fisher's tea with cyanide. Unless… had Jerry been joking about the powder in his cupboard?

Belinda fingered through the contents of her purse until she found van Rooyen's card with his number on it. She wanted to call him straight away, but she didn't want to see him until she had disposed of the cocaine.

The money was fabulous – far more than she had expected. It would pay for first-class air tickets, or a big mansion like this one, or years and years of idle living at Jerry's side.

Transaction completed, Belinda almost asked the drug dealer whether she could use the phone. She checked herself just in time. Walking in Johannesburg might be considered careless – using a drug lord's phone to call the police would definitely prove detrimental.

She walked to her car, wondering where the nearest pay phone was. Perhaps she could get van Rooyen to take her out to dinner. Belinda was confident she could extract the information she craved over a chocolate soufflé.

Suddenly she felt a grip of steel on her elbow. Her scream froze in her lungs.

"Just take the money and go," she whispered, too frightened to regret the newly-acquired riches, too stunned to realise that she had committed – may have committed – murder for nothing.

"Pardon?"

The arm holding her was clad in police uniform.

"I want to speak to Detective van Rooyen," Belinda exhaled with relief.

"You will, sugar. All in good time," replied van Rooyen's partner. "Meanwhile, you are under arrest for the murder of Alexander Richard Fisher. Anything you say…"

Yvonne Walus

Yvonne Eve Walus has lived on three continents and her books reflect the wealth of her cultural background. Published in USA and in Britain, her crime fiction includes 'Murder @ Work' and 'Murder @ Play', both set in the tumultuously exotic South Africa (amazon.com, fictionwise.com). Please visit Yvonne on http://yewalus.kiwiwebhost.net.nz/.

First Impressions

Tricia watched through the car windows as the scenery changed. Soon the concrete grey of the London main roads was replaced by country lanes. Greys became greens.

If only she could relax. Her stomach was churning so much. All she was doing was going to meet James's parents. Why did it have to feel so scary?

"Are you all right love, only you've gone very quiet."

She forced a smile. "I'm fine, James. How soon will be there?"

"In about an hour, maybe less."

She must have frowned.

"Don't look so worried. My parents aren't going to eat you."

"I know," she said. "I'll feel better once we've arrived."

She wondered what was wrong with her. She was in love with a wonderful man, they were getting married in six months; she should be feeling happy. Instead, a feeling of all pervading gloom had settled over her like a black cloud. Questions kept racing through her mind. What if his parents don't like me? What if they think it's all too sudden?

She sighed. However many questions she answered there was always another queue forming, ready to jump into her head.

* * *

Gloria looked at the clock.

"It's five minutes since you last checked the time," joked her husband. "Now come on, relax. It's not the

Queen who's coming to stay. It's just James's fiancée."

"Just James's fiancée. How can you say that?" asked Gloria in amazement. "We haven't even met this girl and suddenly they're getting married. What if she's not right for him? She works in a beauty parlour for goodness sake."

Howard frowned. "And what's wrong with that?"

"Nothing, it's just….." she didn't say any more. She wanted her son to be happy, what the girl did as a job didn't really matter. "I'm sorry," she said. "I guess I'm worried in case we don't get on."

"Well stop worrying," said Howard. "They'll be here soon."

*   *   *

The roads narrowed. Trees were replaced by tall dark hedges.

Tricia's unease grew. Even the landscape was strange. She had no idea how different it would be. She'd been to Devon many times as a child, but they'd always stayed near the sea, never venturing more than a few miles inland. She glanced across at James. He looked as relaxed and happy as she was tense.

"We're here," he said at last, as with practised ease he swung the car into a wide drive. "Come on, we can fetch the luggage later."

She stepped cautiously out of the car and gazed up at the house. Several wide steps led up to an imposing front door. It looked enormous, easily twice the size of her parents' terraced house in West London. She took a deep breath. Even the air smelled different. Crisp and fresh.

James turned the key and stepped into the hall. "Come on."

"I'm not sure about this. Shouldn't we ring the bell,

let them know we're here?"

He laughed. "This is my home, silly. I don't need to ring the bell."

She followed him into the hall. The first thing she noticed was a grandfather clock. It was almost seven feet tall, but it didn't look out of place. Everything was so big – the hallway, the doors. Even the ceiling was high.

James took her hand. "Mum and Dad will be in the kitchen. It's the heart of the house."

She let herself be led along.

The smell of fresh baked bread smothered her as the door swung wide.

James's mother rushed over and gave her son a big hug, then she turned towards Tricia.

Tricia hesitated. Her family didn't go in for big displays of affection. Unsure of what to do, she held out her hand instead. There was a long moment of awkward silence.

James's father laughed. "Don't go frightening the girl, Gloria. Good to see you both," he said as he put an arm on his son's shoulder. "Let's you and me go and get your luggage while your mother shows Tricia to her room."

Gloria led her to a bedroom at the back of the house. It had huge windows looking out on to a panoramic view across fields, complete with cows and sheep. As she looked round the light and airy room she was reminded of a page from a glossy magazine. There were freshly cut anemones on the dressing table, lovely paintings on the walls and a carpet so thick it felt as though she was floating on air. Everything was colour matched. Even the flowers were just the right shade of blue, so that they blended in seamlessly.

It was so breathtakingly wonderful that she couldn't

think of a single word to say.

Just then James and his father appeared in the doorway with her suitcase. "My room's just across the landing," James told her.

"I'll leave the two of you to get settled in," Gloria said, as she took her husband's arm. "Come down when you're ready, and we'll have tea."

"Thanks, Mum," said James

Tricia didn't say anything. She was still gazing at the huge room.

When they were alone, she snuggled up to James "This room is fabulous. I can't believe how big it is. I could get lost in that wardrobe; it's like something out of Narnia."

He laughed. "I suppose it IS a big room. I've never really thought about it before."

"You would if you were a girl with three sisters. I've always had to share."

He laughed again and held her tighter. "So how are you feeling? Butterflies settled down yet?"

She nodded. "A bit. But I won't be able to eat much. My stomach's still feeling unsettled."

"You and your nerves," he said. "Come on, let's get unpacked and then you and my folks can get properly acquainted."

*   *   *

"Well! I don't know what to make of her, Howard. I mean most people say something. You know, what a lovely room, or they mention the view." She frowned. "It took me ages getting it all ready."

"Now now Gloria. She's probably tired. It's a long journey from West London. Anyway, I'm sure she'll appreciate your cooking. " He finished cutting the rich fruit cake into large slabs and took it through into the living room.

He offered the cake round.

"Thanks," said James, taking the biggest slice. He smiled warmly at his mother. "I really miss your cooking."

Gloria soaked up her son's compliments like a sponge. She didn't hold with fussy eaters. Good food, plenty of sleep. That's all anyone needed to stay healthy. None of this faddy nonsense for her.

She glanced at Tricia. The girl was much too thin for her liking, and she wouldn't even try the cake. And what about her nails! They must have cost a fortune. Gloria glanced at her own hands. She never bothered with nail polish. Manicures indeed!

*   *   *

Tricia felt completely overwhelmed. James's parents were so nice. It was a terrible word, but she couldn't think of a better one.

The house was bright and warm, and smelt of bread and cakes. It was all so perfect. She wriggled her toes in her shoes, longing to take them off and nestle her feet into the thick pile of the carpet, but she didn't think her future in laws would approve.

Things didn't improve by the evening meal.

She wasn't allowed to help, not even by laying the table.

"You're our guest," Gloria said sternly. But Tricia didn't feel like a guest. She felt like an alien, dropped into a world totally different from anything she was used to.

When they were alone for a moment, she confided in James. "Everything's so grand here. Look at the table. I'm surprised it's not creaking under the weight of all the cutlery."

He laughed. "It's not always like this. Mum's just trying to make a good impression."

Tricia couldn't help wishing she'd stop trying so hard. She was already impressed. The food looked great but there was too much of it for her fragile nerves to face. She did her best but couldn't clear her plate.

"So what do you think of Mum's cooking? Great, isn't it?"

She smiled and agreed with him, but she noticed Gloria's look of disapproval as the plates were cleared away. Her offer to help with the washing up was met with another, very firm, refusal.

"This is your holiday," Gloria insisted. "James tells me how hard you work, so while you're with us, you must take it easy."

But Tricia didn't feel comfortable taking it easy.

Later, she tried to join in the conversation but by the time she'd thought of something interesting to say, the subject changed. She felt like an extra on a film set, waiting for her cue to speak, but nobody had given her any lines. It was a relief when the TV was turned on for the late evening news.

The next day she didn't feel much better.

"I'm sorry James," she said when he came in to check on her. "I can't face breakfast this morning."

"That's fine. You stay there. I'll get you a cup of tea."

When he came back, he was patting his stomach. "Mum made me eat your breakfast too," he said. "Come on, let's go for a drive. I'll show you the sights."

"Can we go to the seaside? I might feel better if we go somewhere more familiar."

He took her to Paignton. They went on the pier

where they played all kinds of silly games. Then they ate fish and chips, sitting side by side on the sea wall.

Tricia breathed a big deep sigh. This was more like it, the smell of seaweed, the sound of the sea. This was what she was used to, not a polished, sparkling house where she was scared to touch anything.

"You OK?" asked James.

She nodded. "It's all a bit overwhelming. I'm not sure your Mum likes me very much."

"Course she does. What's the matter, darling? You look worried."

"You're so close to your parents. What happens if I can't get on with them?"

He put his arm round her shoulders and pulled her close. "I love you, and I love my Mum and Dad. Once they see how much you mean to me, they'll love you too. Just wait and see."

"I hope so," said Trish as she rested her head on his shoulders, but she wasn't convinced.

*　　*　　*

Back at the house, Howard poured his wife a sherry. "You look like you could use one of these," he said.

She managed a thin smile "Thanks "

"So come on. Tell me what's wrong."

She sat down on the sofa. "It's Tricia. She seems so tense and uncomfortable here, like she can't wait to get away."

"Maybe she's nervous."

"So am I! My son's going to marry this girl and I don't even know who she is."

Howard sat down next to her. "It's going to happen whatever we think, but I'll say this, you don't need a crystal ball to see how much he loves her."

"He never could hide his feelings could he?" Gloria laughed and snuggled closer to her husband. "But I'm worried. I can't see her wanting a family. It would ruin her figure."

"Gloria! They haven't even got married yet."

"Sorry, but I'd love to be a Granny. I just can't see Tricia wanting children. She's so uptight."

"I expect it's just nerves. It can't be easy, meeting us, being in strange surroundings, eating strange food."

"There's nothing strange about my food," Gloria snapped, pretending to be offended.

"I know, you're a great cook." Howard kissed the top of her head, "but you can be a bit ..."

"A bit what?" she demanded.

"Frightening," he pulled a scary face, his eyes wide and staring.

"Nonsense!" she said, slapping her husband playfully on the arm. "I'm an old softie. Everybody knows that. Who could be scared of me?"

*   *   *

In Paignton, the weather changed; the wintery sunshine replaced by persistent rain.

"It's still early," said James. "We could call on my Auntie. I promised to take you round and show you off if we had time."

"I don't know if I can face any more of your relatives," said Tricia. "Not yet anyway."

"You'll love Aunt Em. Trust me. She's about as different from my mother as it's possible to be."

He was right.

The moment she stepped inside Aunt Emily's house Tricia felt at home.

"Good to meet you. Now put your coat over the ban-

190

isters," the older lady said, "there's a dear. Then come and help me get the tea."

The kitchen was small but it was bright and airy. It wasn't immaculately clean and tidy like it was at the Willows. There was some washing up in the sink, and breadcrumbs on the board. She relaxed at once. Even when Aunt Emily threw questions at her she was able to answer them with ease.

"So how are you getting on with my sister?" Emily asked.

"Fine."

The older lady looked at her and pulled a face. "Now my dear, you don't have to pretend with me. I know what she's like. I bet the house has been tidied and polished half to death."

Tricia nodded.

"And I bet she got the best silver out too."

Tricia nodded again.

"And the plates? Don't tell me she used those fancy ones? You can see through them, they're so thin."

Tricia laughed. "I was almost too frightened to drink out of the cups in case I broke them."

"Dear Gloria. She's been so worried about your visit. I told her, relax, be yourself, but she wouldn't listen. She was terrified in case you didn't like her."

"SHE'S been worried?"

"Of course. Hasn't slept for days. Didn't James tell you?"

"No."

He shrugged. "I thought you knew."

Tricia smiled and gave Aunt Emily a hug. "Thank you," she said. "Thank you so much." And then she started to laugh.

"What's so funny?" asked James.

"I've been so terrified your Mother wouldn't like me. I had no idea she might be feeling the same way."

On their way back to the Willows, Tricia noticed an off licence. She asked James to stop and went inside and bought some bottles of wine.

As they crossed the threshold, Tricia still felt nervous, but this time she knew she could cope. She gave the wine to James's father then marched straight into the kitchen

"Right. Now I'm going to help you get dinner ready, and I won't take no for an answer."

Later that evening, as Gloria washed and she wiped, Tricia told her how she'd been feeling. "I was so worried about meeting you, I could hardly eat."

"I'm sorry," replied Gloria. "I wanted everything to be perfect. I guess I just overdid it a bit."

Tricia laughed. "I've been too frightened to touch anything."

"And I thought with your nails, you wouldn't want to." The older woman paused. "About your nails. They look fabulous. Don't they break all the time?"

"No. If they're done right, they last for ages. Did you want me to do yours sometime?"

"Good gracious no, you're on holiday." Tricia raised her eyebrows and Gloria laughed. "Maybe another time, thanks."

For a few minutes the two women worked together in silence, each lost in their own thoughts.

At last Tricia spoke again. "Sorry about missing breakfast this morning. I was too tense to eat."

"You certainly ate enough this evening. How do you keep so thin?"

She shrugged. "I guess I'm just lucky."

"I was skinny once, but then the children came

along," Gloria indicated her expanded waistline.

"But kids are worth it, aren't they? James and I can hardly wait to start a family."

Gloria smiled. Her first impressions had been way off the mark. She and Tricia were going to get along great after all. "Come on, let's go back and join the men. It's time to open another bottle of wine."

Linda Lewis

Linda Lewis (a.k.a. Catherine Howard) is a full-time writer of fiction and non-fiction. She has so many ideas she hardly knows what to do with them. Her short stories are published in UK magazines such as *Take a Break*, as well as in Australia and Scandinavia. She has an agent (Broo Doherty) who is seeking a publisher for her first novel.

Web site – www.lindatorbay.co.uk and www.writespace.co.uk.

No Smoking Please

"You still serious about giving up then?"

Steve looks across at his colleague who is silently releasing wisps of grey smoke through his nostrils.

"I don't really think I have a choice Barry, the wife's been ranting on for ages about my smoking contaminating the children's lungs"

"You smoke around your kids?" asks Barry astonished

"My missus wouldn't let me get away with that, I'm not even allowed to smoke in the garden!"

Steve smiles at Barry who has just lit up his second cigarette in 15 minutes.

"It was different before we started a family, Stephanie never seemed my cigarette butts or the smell, but now she's like a lioness protecting her cubs."

Steve reflects on how things have changed. Stephanie had always known he was a smoker, indeed she'd often shared the odd puff or two. Now her frequent warnings such as "Get your filthy smoke out of the house" or "Do you realize how much your habit is costing us?" seemed all too commonplace. He couldn't quite remember when his smoking had become a necessity. It all started at college and got more serious at university. Now this once harmless bit of pleasure was threatening to rip his marriage apart..

"I love my family too much to let this weed destroy everything"

His friend nods in sympathy.

"Don't blame you mate, only wish I had the guts to kick the habit"

"Look, I'll catch you later, better get back Barry"

Steve stubs out the remaining embers, his line manager will be livid if he leaves it any longer. He hurries back inside the office, hoping that his presence hasn't been too sorely missed.

The Boss Lady is not impressed

"We've had several calls in the last 15 minutes which you could have handled, really Steven I'm not sure you're pulling you weight at the moment!"

There's a look of disgust in her eyes. Steve wishes he could just bury himself in a hole and hide.

"Look I'm really sorry Melanie, I promise I'll make it up to the team"

He feebly hopes this might help to disperse the tension which has built up since he the room. Melanie simply gives him a withering look and returns to her computer console.

Over Lunch break in the canteen Steve pulls a newspaper cutting from out of his pocket. "**Quit Your Habit for Good**" it reads. "**Free NHS funded scheme for those wanting to give up for good**"

He bolts down the rest of his sandwich and heads outside, but not to the usual 'Smoker's Corner'. He carries on out of the industrial complex to a nearby park where he's guaranteed a little more privacy. Finally seated on an empty bench, hands trembling, Steve pulls out his mobile and dials the NHS helpline number from the advertisement.

"Er, Hi .. Is this the Smoke Free Support Group?"

An intense sensation of both fear and embarrassment begins to overwhelm him. A friendly voice replies.

"Yes, are you interested in joining us?"

Steve hesitates briefly before answering

"I'd like to give it a go"

He feels the unpleasant sensation of a few moments

ago begin to lift a little.

"You're doing the right thing" is the encouraging reply.

A brief discussion about times, dates and locations ensues which appear to be flexible enough for Steve fit into the juggling act of work and family commitments.

A feeling of relief surges through him as he realizes that he's just taken the first step to freedom. Now filled with a new determination to succeed, he returns to the office, and even manages to go through the whole afternoon without the familiar craving for nicotine. Even Melanie notices his abstinence.

"You're in a good mood, won the lottery did we?" she sniggers.

"No, just figured out that life is for living!"

Melanie who clearly wasn't expecting this response flashes him one of her rare smiles.

"Good work today Steven, See you tomorrow."

Steve glances furtively at the clock on the office wall,

"*4.45pm ! My God she's actually letting me go early!*"

Feeling chuffed with himself, Steve tidies up his desk, hoping that he might just make the earlier bus and be in Stephanie's good books as well. On the way out he bumps into Barry who is having one final drag before setting off.

"You off early then Steve, didn't see you at break this afternoon"

Barry adds sounding a little disappointed.

"Nah, might as well resign myself to the fact that it's all or nothing"

"Bet you won't stick it", Barry jeers at him.

Steve feels a sense of foreboding begin to grip like

an icy hand round his chest, but remembering the friendly voice of the girl on the phone he manages to utter

"Well, I'm giving it my best shot. Better go mate, bus to catch!"

Steve walks away briskly, just the smell of Barry's nicotine infused smoke is enough to drive him berserk with longing, and he still has to wait in that dammed queue without a ciggie to console him.

Steve arrives at the bus stop in the rain to find a depressingly long queue of commuters all vying for a place under the shelter. The cravings for a nicotine fix are beginning to build up inside him.

"Don't do it, keep calm, focus on something else"

Steve finds his attention drawn to a rather striking red felt hat, decorated with a nest of silver tinsel. This festive head piece is set off by the thoughtful addition of a small Robin on top. Its wearer is an elderly lady, at least in her eighties Steve surmises. She starts scratching around in her handbag as in the distance, the bus can be seen chugging it's way up the high street. The bus draws to a halt, and the long snake of passengers begin to clamber on board. The poor woman has become quite distressed by this point.

"I… I can't find me tokens"

Steve hears her anguished wail. This does not impress the bus driver who hasn't the time or the patience to deal with her dilemma.

"That'll be £3.50 then my dear"

"I don't collect my pension till Thursday" She protests, shaking with anxiety.

"Sorry Love, but if you ain't got your tokens, you'll have to pay cash"

The remaining few left in the queue begin to shuffle

about with irritation.

"Make that two fares please!"

Steve thrusts a tenner into the astonished bus driver's hand.

"I'd have only spent it on ciggies anyway" Steve whispers to her.

Her face breaks into a beaming smile.

"God bless you son" She pats Steve affectionately on the arm.

"Here, have a packet of Garibaldi biscuits" She offers as they try to find a seat.

"Thanks but no, got to watch the old waistline" replies Steve, hoping that his refusal won't hurt her feelings. As it turns out there is only one seat available which Steve makes sure goes to his elderly companion. He finds himself longing suddenly for the comfort of his car, now reserved for Stephanie's use.

Ferrying two toddlers around on public transport was not an option she'd declared, and they could do without having two cars to run.

"Awful weather we're having isn't it!, I'm Doris by the way" His new friend introduces herself.

"Pleased to meet you Doris, I'm Steve – Nice hat by the way"

"Oh this old thing! We had our over 60's annual Christmas Dinner today at the Salvation Army Centre, won a prize for it I did!"

She pauses to get a better look him. .

"I have son called Steve too, he's in the Police Force you know" she adds proudly. "What line of business are you in?"

"Oh nothing as heroic, Finance, Accounting, that sort of thing"

"Never hurts to have a good head for figures, that's

my failing I'm afraid, not very good at keeping records on my spending" she chuckles.

Steve is quite unaccustomed to having the opportunity of having such friendly conversation with a total stranger, yet alone a batty old lady half a Christmas tree on her head. Nevertheless he finds himself keen to learn more about her.

"How about you Doris, what kind of work did you do"

"My Patty wouldn't let me have a proper job, said I had enough to do looking after the house and the kids. I used to do dressmaking on the side when my family were grown up." Her eyes turn a little misty as she reflects on happier days. Steve smiles, trying to imagine the colourful creations she must have come up with.

"And your Husband, what did he do for a living?" Steve asks gently

"He was a fireman, very brave man but not brave enough to kick his smoking habit. Gone now I'm afraid, died of lung cancer five years ago….I always think if he'd been able to stop earlier I'd still have him today. Oh just listen to me ranting on, must be boring you. Do you have a wife and family Steve?" she enquires, eager to change the subject.

Steve's face lights up "Yes Harry, he's five and Lucy she's just turned three, quite a handful". Steve loved to talk about his family. He'd always liked to think of himself as one of those 'Hands on Dads', not afraid to change nappies or help at bath times.

"And your wife…"

Doris seemed as keen as himself to find out a little more about personal backgrounds.

"Stephanie was a Primary School Teacher before she had the children. We're lucky that she's been able to take a career break to be with them while they're this young"

Doris obviously approved of this idea.

"I bet your two are much better behaved because of it. This is the trouble with the young people these days, there's not enough discipline at home!"

Steve nods in agreement. It was true, he and Stephanie had been fortunate with their kid's behaviour in general.

At this point Steve is struck by how easy Doris seems to talk to. It's almost as if he's known her all his life. She isn't that dissimilar to his Father's Mother, who died when he was only seven.

"I always say that your family should be your most "

"Treasured possession" Steve finishes her sentence off for her.

At that moment it's as if time has come to a stand still. Doris looks him directly in the eye. He can feel her gaze reaching into his soul.. She silently takes his hand.

"Nice to have met you young man. I'd like to thank you for spending your time and money on an old lady like me"

"My pleasure" is all Steve manages to reply before a shrill ringing starts from inside his jacket pocket.

"Excuse me Doris" Steve turns around to answer the call.

"Hi it's me" Stephanie's voice sounds a little strained.

"I wondered if you could call in to the supermarket on your way home, I desperately need more mincemeat for my mincepies. It's the kid's School Christmas Party tomorrow, and I can't face dragging them out again."

Steve sighs inwardly. The last thing he wants to do is trundle round a supermarket at this time of night. "Yeah sure, anything else you need?"

"No, just don't be too long ok?"

"Sorry about that" Steve starts to say as he realizes that Doris' seat is now empty.

How did she manage that? He was certain no one had got on or off the bus in the last 20 seconds.

"You gonna sit in that seat or just stare at it?"

Demands a rather inebriated man dressed in what must be some poor excuse for a Santa Claus outfit.

"All yours mate" Steve replies as he makes his way towards the exit.

During the next few minutes he ponders over the things Doris had mentioned about her son Steve being a Policeman, but Dad's name is Peter and he's worked in the construction industry all his life. Dad did have a brother whom they never met, due to some stupid family rift years before Dad got married. Something about his brother being the family favourite.

"*I must be going nuts, there's no way I could have just met the ghost of my deceased Grandmother, still Grandad did die from lung cancer, and Mum says he smoked worse than a chimney*"

The urge to ditch his smoking addiction suddenly became a little stronger.

Steve finally alights at his stop and heads for the su-permarket store. Normally the first thing he'd have done would be to queue up at the kiosk and ask for a packet of ciggies, but not this time. He strides purposefully to the area where he hopes he'll find a jar of mincemeat. Feeling proud of his self discipline has lightened his mood. The flower stand is near the checkout. Acting on impulse he selects a bunch of pale pink roses, some of which are still in bud. "*Steph will love these*"

Steve reaches the front door step and as soon as he jangles his keys in the lock, he hears the excited cries of Harry.

"Daddy's home!"

An excited five year old rushes up the hallway, almost knocking Steve off his feet with a massive hug. "Daddy, daddy Mummy's making your favourite Chilly Canny for tea!"

"Chilli con Carne, Sweetheart,"

"What are those flowers for Daddy?"

Harry has spotted the bouquet under his arm.

"These are for your Mummy" he says secretively

Stephanie appears in the hallway, with a tired looking Lucy in her arms who judging from the smears of flour on her cheeks has been attempting to help Stephanie with her baking.

"Hi. You're back in good time, and flowers! What's the special occasion"

Her face is a mixture of surprise and suspicion.

"I'm giving it up, I've thought it through and I think the timing's just right"

Steve announces boldly.

His news does not appear to have the effect he was hoping for as Stephanie suddenly wheels round and heads for the kitchen.

"What have I done wrong now!"

"So you think you can just jack it in without even consulting me, what are we all supposed to live on!" Stephanie demands icily.

"No no You've got it all wrong. I'm not quitting my job, I'M QUITTING SMOKING!"

Stephanie's face relaxes into a beaming smile. "That's brilliant Darling!"

She comes over to give him a cuddle, placing Lucy

on his lap.

"I'm so proud of you"

Lucy who is by now fully awake has been paying more attention to the conversation than they realized. "Does that mean Daddy won't smell funny anymore?"

Steve is appalled that his child has noticed that much.

"I hope all I ever smell of is my aftershave!"

"I hope that hacking cough of yours will disappear too" Stephanie teases.

"Hey, this is not the kind of encouragement I was hoping to receive. It's going to be tough you know!" Steve grumbles.

"Oh sorry, poor thing. Kids, do you think Daddy deserves an extra big helping of Chilli?"

"Yes!" They both chorus.

Steve feels slightly more placated with this response.

"We are going to have to give your Daddy a lot more TLC from now on"

Harry's face creases with concentration. " TLC, Tasty Lumps of cheese?" he enquires.

"No that's Tender Loving Care" Steve replies as the largest helping of Chilli con Carne he has ever seen is placed before him.

Wendy Busby

Wendy Busby has been writing poems for friends and family since she was a child. With help and support from her local creative writing group she is now experimenting with short stories for young people.

Sally and the Sign People

Chapter One

My name is Sally and I live by the sea.

It's my home. And by the way, I'm a seagull. Although, science bit coming up... are you concentrating? What do you mean, no! Tough. Here it comes. Officially, there is no such thing as a seagull. It's a commonly used name to describe all the different types of gulls who live near the sea. Lesson over.

Where am I supposed to live? London? And catch the tube every morning while carrying my little briefcase under one wing. Or, perhaps I should move to the North Pole? Be a bit cold with only my feathers to keep me warm.

Do I sound a little angry? That's probably because I am.

It all began the other day. I was on the seafront waiting for Mrs Harris and her sardine sandwiches. My favourite! They were meant for me. Mrs Harris had made that very plain.

"Come here my feathered friends," she called out. "Let's be having you."

I was about to pick up a tasty-looking piece when a dog sprinted past me so fast I spun round on the spot. I looked like my baby brother's spinning top.

And whoever heard of a dog eating sardine sandwiches anyway? What kind of strange dog was that? Whatever next – pear drops and ice cream sundaes?

Had he been hiding up a palm tree?

"Hey!" I said. "What were you doing – hiding up a palm tree?"

I glared at him not that he took any notice. He was

too busy gulping down *my* sandwiches. I squawked and fluttered above him. He didn't so much as wag his tail in reply. Too busy enjoying what was now left of *my* sandwiches.

It's hard enough with all those signs along the seafront asking people to: "Kindly refrain from feeding the seagulls as they are a nuisance."

Nuisance! Charming, that is. I like that. Who's a nuisance? And what does refrain mean? I asked my granddad when I got home and he told me it's a human way of saying stop.

Sometimes, it's hard being a seagull.

The fishermen don't want us near them and their catch of the day, the sign people don't want us mingling with the tourists along the seafront.

Where else should we go to get a decent meal? It's not as if we can ring up on our mobile phones and book a table at the local fish and chip restaurant or pop out for a takeaway. We'd end up *on* the menu.

What does a seagull have to do?

The other day, I found myself a big juicy worm... what do you mean, poor thing. A seagull has to eat. Anyway, it was dead when I found it. Even worms get old and die. (All right, I admit the sight of my open beak flying in his direction might have brought on a heart attack) when a cheeky robin flew by and grabbed it from my mouth. Nearly had a tug of war going on. Most undignified it was.

He only got away with it because he caught me unawares.

I mean, when you sit down to enjoy a spot of breakfast you don't expect it to be seized by some bird that gets his picture on cards and wrapping paper once a year.

He thinks he's a supermodel or something.

It's all right to feed robins. Of course, it is, they're

dinky and cute. The sign people will happily share a meal or two with a supermodel... but when it comes to a sea-gull... that's a different story.

What am I supposed to do? Shrink myself and paint my feathers red? All right, I agree, he is kind of cute.

Talking of cute, I met a gorgeous gull the other day. I found out his name is Saxon Seagull. He's named after a famous rock group. No, not like Stonehenge or Land's End, a musical rock group.

His uncle used to play heavy metal. He's a doctor now, Dr Sigmund Seagull. Although, what's so interesting about tractors and bits of rusty iron and what's that got to do with music... I do not know.

Anyway, I'm getting sidetracked from telling you how I met Saxon.

I was sitting on my favourite rock over at Sennen Cove keeping an eye open for a fish or two, when all of a sudden this good-looking gull flies right past me.

Fascinated, I watched, as he dive-bombed into the water and flew out again with a fish clasped within his beak without so much as a feather ruffled.

What did he do then? He only hops over to where I'm hovering with my beak hanging open (that was cool, Sally) winks at me and drops the fish inside my mouth! Nothing like that has ever happened to me before. It was *so* romantic.

And he was wearing one of those portable CD play-ers, a waterproof one of course. Lucky bird. I've always wanted one of those.

If I had a CD player, I could listen to all my favourite pop groups whenever I wanted. I could even listen to that group from the eighties called A Flock of Seagulls.

I know that's like a million years ago, but my great, great, great, great (I don't know how many greats... lots and lots, I know that much) grandparents were around when the group was big and famous and performed all over the world.

The humans named the group after my great, great, great, great (lots and lots of greats) grandparents, so I'm sort of related to the group, in a funny sort of way.

It's my small claim to fame. That is… and Granddad.

Anyway, Saxon Seagull is way cool. Now I always make sure I'm looking my best in case I bump into Saxon again.

Not that I would dream of setting one webbed foot outside our nest without my favourite choker or my beak stud. It's only a clip on. The beak stud. Granddad would go mad if I went and had a hole punched through my beak… wouldn't much fancy it myself to be honest.

Makes my stomach go all wobbly just thinking about it.

Saffron, she's my best friend, she said she's going to get her beak pierced but I think she's bluffing. I think she said that to impress the gulls from the other side of the cliffs.

They think they're cool. They wear sunglasses and anklets made out of seaweed. They're okay, I guess. Although, not as cool as Saxon. No one's as cool as Saxon… except my granddad.

Granddad's not only the number one flier around these parts but he's also an actor! Or, he was. He's retired now. He used to perform at the Minack Theatre – the famous open-air theatre here in Cornwall.

He's starred with some of the biggest names in show business… such as Merle Ostrich in *Wuthering Heights,* Kestrel Winslet in *Titanic* and he performed in a pop video with Kittiwake Minogue. He thought she was very nice but spent far too much time fluffing up her tail feathers.

He doesn't let anything get in his way. Granddad's really brave.

Many years ago, he found himself trapped in an old and forgotten fishing net. It can be very dangerous for the creatures that live in the sea never mind gulls. Anyway, Granddad was stuck fast like in a steel trap, but he wasn't about to give up. Using all his strength and lots of wriggling, he managed to escape with his life but lost his foot in the process. Not that it matters one little bit. Nobody needs legs when they're flying except perhaps when they land. The landings can get a bit bumpy.

Sometimes he looks more like a rabbit hopping along than a seagull coming in to land.

It was Granddad who taught me how to tap dance on the grass. We do it to fool the worms, to make them think it's raining… and when they pop their heads up from out of the ground… well… you can guess the rest. Not such a happy ending for the worm, but a seagull has to eat.

I'm not sure what I want to do when I grow up. I might take up acting or become an explorer like my mum and dad. That's why Granddad looks after George, my younger brother, and me. My parents are away exploring different territories along the coast in case we have to move on.

Like I said, it's hard being a seagull.

I'm glad not everyone thinks like the sign people. The tourists love us. Only the other day I overheard a nice lady talking to Mr Trewellan in his shop.

"I love to hear the screech of a seagull because then I know I'm near to the sea," she said to Mr Trewellan who was busy wrapping up two strawberry crumble cakes I'd had my eye on all morning.

At least the tourists appreciate us and Penzance depends on tourists and not only Penzance but all the other seaside towns too. And that's when I got my idea... a brilliant idea.

Well, at least *I* thought it was brilliant!

Chapter Two

I told Saffron all about it.

We were sitting on the granite rocks out at Land's End.

"Oh, I don't know, Sally," she said while preening her feathers. "Isn't it a little bit dangerous?"

"Of course not," I replied.

"What does your granddad say?"

"I haven't told him yet," I replied as I fiddled with my headscarf. It's exactly like the one that Spice Bird wears, Vulture Beckham.

"Won't he find out about it?"

"Yes," I replied. "Soon," I added.

In fact, he found out a lot sooner than that – the very next day. Granddad was hopping mad. Literally. He looked like a pneumatic drill.

"Sally Seagull," he spluttered. "I don't know where you get your hare-brained ideas from, I really don't."

I looked down as I traced my foot in the sand.

"George didn't mind," I answered.

"George is too young to know what he wants."

"Nothing happened."

"It could have though, all sorts of things could have happened."

Why are adults always concerned about what *could* have happened? It didn't, so where's the problem. Humans could get run over crossing the road but they still cross it, don't they? They cross it *but* they're careful while

209

they're doing it.

"I'm responsible for you and George, you should have told me about your plans, Sally."

"I was being careful, Granddad," I said while standing there looking suitably told off and sorry and I promised never to do anything like it again.

"I promise, Granddad."

What was it that I'd done? I'd put on a show of fancy flying and aerobatics in front of the tourists.

Whoosh! I flew in low over George and then whoosh! Together we weaved in and out of the palm leaves, called fronds, on one of the many palm trees found standing along the seafront like soldiers on parade.

And guess what we did for the big finale?

I climbed up high in the sky to free-fall all the way back down to earth again. The tourists loved it. They clapped and cheered and we were having a great time until the sign people arrived.

The moment I saw them waving their arms about I made sure George was well out of the way. I'd never let anything happen to him.

I wanted to show the sign people how much the tourists love us.

"I wanted to show them, Granddad," I said.

"I know, Sally. You're a good girl. It's simply that I don't trust those sign people, you don't know what they are capable of."

"Back to the drawing board then, Granddad?"

"I'm afraid so, my lovely, I'm afraid so."

I stood there looking thoughtful for a moment and then said. "What's for dinner tonight, Granddad? Can I help?"

"That's my girl," he smiled. "A bit of swordfish if I can find any unless," he looked up from polishing his glasses, "unless you'd like to catch a few mackerel over in Sennen Cove?"

Sennen Cove? You mean, the same Sennen Cove where Saxon hangs out? Let me think about this… not. I was out of there in seconds flat. After I'd fixed and preened my feathers first, of course.

A few minutes later and I was circling above looking down at the little cove nestled amongst the granite rocks and rows of cottages set further back. They looked tiny, barely big enough for a seagull to live in let alone a human. Of course they are much larger close up.

The sea splashed against the rocks sending a shower of water high in the air and all over me. I wasn't having much luck. It looked like the fishermen had beaten me to it, again, although I wasn't about to give up. I knew a mackerel would swim along before too long.

I flew up and away to land squarely on the roof of The Round House and Capstan Gallery (it sells such pretty things and I know because I've peeped in through their window). I hopped about until I found a comfortable spot on which to perch and shook off the last few droplets of water.

I sat there for what felt like forever. Dreaming of Saxon. Wondering what I would say to him when I accidentally on purpose bumped into him... when a sudden movement startled me out of my daydreams.

Who do you think was gliding skillfully across the water towards me like a Red Arrow? Granddad. And guess who was with him? I felt myself blush as red as that cheeky worm stealing robin.

It was Saxon.

Chapter Three

Granddad was shouting something, but with the noise of the waves crashing against the rocks, I could only make out the odd word.

"… worked… success… famous."

Famous? What was he talking about?

"What are you talking about, Granddad?" I shouted across the water.

"… fish and chips…" I caught as he flew right past me. Fish and chips?

With one swift movement Saxon landed beside me. "Come with us, Sally, we have something to show you."

"All right," I replied, blushing.

I didn't know what all the excitement and fuss was about, but I didn't much care. I was about to soar high in the sky with Saxon Seagull. Life didn't get any better.

I was about to find out how wrong I could be.

We flew all the way to the seafront in Penzance before landing. I stood there panting like a dog as I tried to catch my breath. I wasn't used to flying quite so fast.

Saxon waddled over and gently placed his wing on mine. "Are you all right?" he asked with some concern.

"Yes, thanks," I replied blushing to the root of my quills.

"Sally!" Granddad called excitedly as he flew in tiny circles in preparation. It's the only way he can land without bouncing halfway to Devon and back again.

"It worked!" he shouted as he hopped over to where I was standing next to Saxon.

"What worked, Granddad?"

"Your plan, it worked after all."

"I don't understand."

"Look!"

I did as I was told and looked in the direction his beak was pointing. I couldn't believe my eyes. I pinched myself to see if I was dreaming. The pinch hurt. It was real. I wasn't asleep and it wasn't a dream.

Saffron was there. So was the cool gang, you know the one I mean… seaweed anklets and wearing sunglasses when the sun isn't even shining.

George was there too, waving excitedly along with all our neighbours and friends.

It was the biggest flock of seagulls I had ever seen.

"The sign people will love this," I giggled.

"The sign people don't have any say in the matter," Granddad replied as he adjusted the cravat he always wore around his neck. Most actors wear them. (It's an actor thing).

"Why? What's going on?"

"Sidney Seagull and his wife, Sophie," Granddad nodded over to where George was nestled protectively in the wings of an older couple, "were strolling along the seafront, as they do every evening before turning in, and came across a newspaper in which were the remains of a portion of fish and chips."

I listened carefully wondering where this was going.

"That's when they saw it."

"Saw what?" I asked.

"Your story in the local newspaper – the tourists rebelled."

"The tourists did what?"

"They rebelled. They said they wouldn't come to Penzance any longer unless the sign people took away their signs and allowed the seagulls to come and go as they pleased. They said it would be unreasonable even to think of having a seafront without any seagulls and they weren't going to stand for it."

"And, it's all because of your flying display," Saxon added.

"My display?"

"Your display," he repeated with a grin.

Sidney took up the story. "The tourists thought the sign people were wrong to chase you and George away," he explained in his rich and gentle voice.

"That's right," added Sophie as she adjusted her necklace of shiny pearls.

"The tourists, along with Mrs Harris and her friends, agreed Penzance would not be the same without its seagulls and that we have a right to be here," said Sidney.

"That's right," Sophie added again.

"They told the sign people that they'd sooner visit other seaside towns where seagulls are welcome. It was their choice," Sidney explained.

I listened with eyes wide open. Humans standing up for the rights of seagulls? I mean, wow! That was a nice change. It made me feel wonderful and very humble both at the same time.

"The sign people were made to realise they were behaving in an unreasonable manner..."

"What's unreasonable?" George piped up.

"Stupid," I replied.

"I only asked," George answered crossly.

"No! Unreasonable means stupid or pointless," I laughed and tweaked a tuft of his baby feathers.

"... and if it continued, they'd not only have no seagulls on the seafront, but no tourists either," Sidney paused. "They had to reconsider and do what was best for Cornwall and everyone concerned. Including the seagulls."

"Granddad, does this mean you're not angry with me anymore?"

214

"I was never angry with you, Sally, only concerned for your safety and that of George's," Granddad replied as he put his wing around me.

"It turned out all right in the end though, didn't it, Granddad?"

"Yes, it did." Granddad answered with a nod before continuing. "And in future, I promise I won't treat you as if you're nothing but a fledgling. You're growing up fast my little Sally, into a remarkable young gull – and I'm proud of you," he added.

I blushed and found the ground the most interesting thing in the world while Granddad furiously began to clean his glasses.

"Now everyone, please gather round and listen." The powerful voice of Sinclair Seagull rang out. He was older than Granddad and was considered to be the wisest of the seagulls.

Sinclair continued. "I suggest to you, my feathered friends, in order to keep things on a happy and harmonious level, we set aside a section for feeding purposes only. How about that grassy area by the palm trees?"

I looked around as a group of heads nodded in agreement.

"That way, we give the sign people no reason to complain and," he spread his wings wide open, "everyone's happy."

We all cheered and squawked in agreement.

"Let's not forget a big cheer for Sally Seagull," he finished.

"And the tourists and Mrs Harris and her friends. And my baby brother," I added as I winked at George.

What a day that turned out to be.

I felt quite the hero. Or, I should say heroine seeing as I am a girl, or a young lady as Granddad now calls me.

I only wished my mum and dad could have been there as well.

Chapter Four

It's been two weeks since that wonderful day.

Mum and Dad are home to stay and ooh! Before I forget. Let me bring you up to date with the latest on Saxon Seagull. He and I are going out together. And, he gave me his most treasured possession – his portable waterproof CD player.

There was me thinking at the rate things were going, I'd be as old as Granddad before I was lucky enough to own one.

"Hello," said Mrs Harris as she fished inside her basket.

I was sitting on the seafront on our very own official eating area waiting for Mrs Harris... and her sardine sandwiches... to arrive. Let's not forget her sandwiches. I'm not just a greedy ball of feathers of course it's nice to see Mrs Harris... and her sardine sandwiches.

Yummy! The best meal in the world next to a Cornish pasty, I thought excitedly, when grumble, grumble! My tummy rumbled. Oops! That was embarrassing. It was so loud I heard it over my headphones.

I screeched in reply and flapped my wings excitedly. I'd been waiting for this moment... this was pure bliss... this... this couldn't be happening... I don't believe it.

It was that pesky stealing sardine sandwich dog again.

"Hello, Buster," Mrs Harris said as she stooped down to pat his head. "Have you and your friend been waiting long?"

Buster? Friend? Who's that? Me! I glared at the four-legged hearthrug.

"There's plenty to go round," she said.

I puffed out my feathers and was about to make my feelings all too clear when a flutter of tiny wings brushed past me.

"Hello, Red Eric," Mrs Harris looked down as she greeted the plump little bird. "I didn't expect to see you here, you've already had a big breakfast."

Red Eric? Big breakfast? What was that?

I looked over at the stealing sardine sandwich dog only to see the stealing sardine sandwich dog looking back at me.

"Woof!"

"Squawk!"

The robin kept on hopping. Ha-ha! Got you this time, supermodel.

Now, can I please eat my sardine sandwich in peace before the hearthrug gobbles them up? I mean, what does a seagull have to do.

What was this?

The hearthrug was walking towards me with something in his mouth. It wasn't the robin, was it? He dropped it on the grass next to my webbed feet. My panic disappears as I recognise a soggy piece of sardine sandwich.

Well, I suppose there is enough to share with, what's his name? Buster? And, perhaps the supermodel can have some too if he learns to be not quite so greedy. I'd spied a blob of red hiding in amongst the palm trees. I think he's sorry for stealing my worm.

Anyway, as long as he and Buster realise we can *only* be friends because, I am spoken for, as my granddad would say in his rich theatrical voice while polishing his reading glasses and adjusting his cravat! (It's an actor thing).

Yes! I am a happy gull... and ooh! Before I double forget. I asked Granddad and he said heavy metal is very loud harsh-sounding rock music with a strong beat.

Granddad said he'd rather listen to rusty tractors... or Kittiwake Minogue.

And between you, me, and the Atlantic sea... so would I.

So, now you know my story.

A story about how our homes were saved (I'm glad we didn't have to move – especially to the North Pole... never did fancy myself much in a fur coat. Would have looked like a cross between a wombat and a penguin). And how humans stood up for seagulls.

Ooh! Is that a worm I spy? It's all right. Keep your hair on, no need to ring the RSPCW (Royal Society for the Prevention of Cruelty to Worms) it's a dead one... or is he asleep... what!

So shoot me. I *am* a seagull.

Rosemary A. Bach-Holzer

Writer, David Renwick, is Rosemary's inspiration as is her grandfather. Her belief that her love of writing and cats runs in the blood leaves Rosemary with a constant fear of a transfusion. Visit Rosemary on her website at:
www.bachchat.fusiveweb.co.uk.

A Present for St Nicolas

St Nicolas was tired. This time of year was always extremely busy but the older he got the quicker December seemed to arrive and the bigger the pile of presents seemed to become. The letters had been streaming in for weeks now and were in the process of being sorted. The 6th of December was looming. Mostly he looked forward to it. It was his big day, after all. The reason he existed as Pete, his assistant, kept pointing out. "If only I had a day named after me," he would grumble. "Always doing things for other people and never getting noticed. But if it wasn't for me they'd all be getting the wrong parcels, the way you've been carrying on these last weeks."

St Nicolas was usually able to cheer him up by promising him the pick of the presents and a slap-up meal at the end of it all, but this year was different. Pete was right. He seemed to have lost his touch, both with customers and colleagues. The trouble was he just couldn't get himself going. And there was so much work to do. Along with the dinosaurs and the dragons and the dolls that could dance, there were stacks of letters asking for Star Wars 6 or Harry Potter 7 and it all had to be compatible with Windows 3000. All these numbers and he never had been good at mathematics. It was making him feel positively dizzy. "More post," grinned Pete, as he dragged in another sack. St Nicolas' heart sank. He wondered what was wrong with him. He hoped he wasn't coming down with something. That would be most unfortunate.

"Let's get going!" Pete tore open another letter and started reading. All the letters were sorted into different piles. The one for computer games had grown so big it had to be moved to another room. Pete frowned. "Now here's a tricky one."

"Miscellaneous, if you have any doubts," said St Nicolas wearily. "Miscellaneous" had started off as a small pile consisting of a doll that could vomit, a boomerang that actually came back and a computer that did your homework for you. Since then it had become such a high pile it was in danger of collapsing and spilling over into 'sports accessories'.

"Listen to this," said Pete, shaking his head.

Dear St Nicolas,
What would YOU like this yeer?
Please choose.
1) a mobile
2) a chocolate st nicolas so you can eet yourself up
3) a holliday

love Laya
PS My bruther thinks you don't exist. Will you tell him that you do?

St Nicolas' eyes lit up. This was the first time in his long, long life that he had received a letter asking him what <u>he</u> would like. He shook his head in delight and grabbed the letter from Pete. He had to read it three times to make sure it wasn't a mistake.

"Bin it!" cried Pete impatiently. They really didn't have the time to stare at every letter for five minutes.

"But this is just what I need," said St Nicolas. "I feel better already."

And then he took a pen and put a tick beside number

3.

"This year," he declared triumphantly, "I am going to take a holiday."

Luke had a plan. A secret plan. He was going to conduct an experiment. He was (almost) certain that St Nicolas didn't exist and this year he was going to keep awake and see just who it was who delivered those presents. The thought made him feel both excited and frightened at the same time.

He wasn't going to tell anybody. Especially not his little sister, Laya. Every time he started to talk about St Nicolas his mum would kick him under the table and frown at him. Sometimes he positively hated having a sister. She was so annoying and she got away with everything. She would pinch his lego and mess up his computer games and he would always get the blame. He was sure his mum liked her better than him. And she was so stupid. She even wrote letters to St Nicolas and posted them with a proper stamp!

On December 5th he inspected the sitting room to find the best spot to hide. Under the sofa would be safe but then he wouldn't be able to see anything. Squeezing into the cupboard would be too risky with all those wine glasses. Behind the curtain under the window looked promising. He would pretend to be asleep when his mum came round and then when he was sure they had all gone to bed he would tiptoe downstairs and install himself behind the curtain in full view of the chimney.

St Nicolas was feeling a little worried. Although he was sure the children would understand that he needed a holiday once in a while he didn't like disappointing them. He would just have to hope the grown-ups would stand in for

221

him this year. He knew how much they enjoyed doing that but still, it was a risky business leaving it up to the adults. They didn't always get it right. And then there was the postscript in the letter that was worrying him. It was going to be difficult to convince someone he existed just the year he was having a holiday.

I know what I'll do, he thought. I'll send them a letter! He was so tickled by the idea he decided to tell Pete at once. It might cheer him up, he thought. He'd been in a mood ever since he'd heard about the holiday. He loved climbing over roofs and sliding down chimneys and was at a loss what to do this year.

"Don't think I'm going to do your delivering for you," grumbled Pete. "I do presents, not letters."

"You don't need to deliver it. It's not a normal sort of letter," said St Nicolas patiently. "At midnight on the 5th December there's going to be the most beautiful snowstorm you've ever seen and my letter is going to tumble through the sky like snow."

"What's the point of that?" muttered Pete. "They'll all be asleep."

"Not all of them. It's for the ones who are awake," said St Nicolas. "And the ones who think I don't exist."

"Humph," grunted Pete. It sounded a poor substitute for all those presents. And not nearly as much fun as walking along telegraph wires or bungee jumping down chimneys.

In the Lawrence household everything seemed to be going according to plan. The shoes had been put out next to the fireplace and Luke noticed how keen his mum seemed to be to get them to bed as early as possible. To keep himself awake Luke had set two alarm clocks, one under his pillow and one in his woolly hat that he was going to wear in bed that night. He had set the first one for 11.30 pm and the other for a quarter to midnight. He surely couldn't sleep through both.

How long a night lasts if you stay awake, thought Luke, looking at his watch. He couldn't believe it was only 10.30pm. He could hear the television droning on in the sitting room downstairs. Surely they weren't going to stay down there till midnight. The next thing he knew there was a loud buzzing in his head as if a bee was trapped in his brain. But then he remembered it was only the alarm in his hat. 11.45pm – thank goodness for that. He tried to turn it off but it seemed to have got tangled in his hair and it took a while to find the right button. By the time he had managed to switch it off he was afraid he had woken the whole street. But there was complete silence all around him. Everyone was still fast asleep. Thank goodness for that. He stood outside his sister's room and heard her breathing steadily.

Luke made his way downstairs as quietly as he could. He could feel his heart beating as loud as his alarm clock. He pushed open the sitting room door and saw the two shoes waiting there patiently in front of the fireplace. Laya had left a carrot and a chocolate St Nicolas in hers and she had put his mum's mobile phone next to it. How stupid can you get! He crept across the carpet and crouched down under the window, enveloping himself in the curtain. He felt suddenly nervous.

What if he actually did turn up? The thought of meeting St Nicolas face to face seemed unexpectedly alarming. But he didn't exist of course, so there was no danger of that. But ... what if he did? What if he came slithering down the chimney and discovered him hiding there like that? Maybe he'd take all the presents back. Or, worse still, perhaps he'd even tie him up in a sack and take him away.

In that instance something brushed against the window. Luke froze. When he looked up he saw the glass was speckled with tiny white crystals. Hundreds of snowflakes were falling from the sky like pieces of torn up paper. His mouth fell open. He'd never seen such beautiful snowflakes. They drummed and swirled in the sky as if they were dancing and then fluttered against the glass like a butterfly, leaving a pattern of ice on the pane. Luke stared. It seemed like a random jumble of letters but when he peered closer it was as if they had left a message on the window. What could it mean? Maybe it was a secret code.

And then he had an idea. Of course he was seeing it back to front. He needed to read it from the outside!

Luke ran to the back door, unlocked it quickly and slipped out into the garden. He couldn't believe his eyes. The sky was pink and everything was covered in a layer of thick, white snow. He didn't recognize his garden anymore. The branches of the trees were transformed into long fingers, dripping with icing sugar. The bushes had turned into huge snowballs, sparkling with diamonds. The snow was so bright he had to blink. The grass had disappeared under a glistening carpet of ice. There wasn't a single footprint. It was as if nobody had ever walked here before. He tiptoed to the window and traced the letters with his fingers.

THANK YOU FOR MY HOLIDAY. BACK NEXT YEAR. ST NICOLAS.

Holiday? That meant he wouldn't be coming after all. Luke felt suddenly as flat as a deflated balloon. His feet were frozen now and he was starting to shiver but he was reluctant to leave the magic of the garden. When he went back inside he took the chocolate St Nicolas out of Laya's shoe and started to eat it. He wouldn't be needing it now. A wave of exhaustion swept over him and he sat down for a moment in the armchair and gazed at the chimney. The next thing he knew his father was carrying him upstairs and his mother was shooing the cat into the garden, complaining that someone hadn't locked the back door. And wasn't that a pile of parcels beside the chimney?

The next day Luke was woken by Laya bouncing on top of him. His head felt fuzzy. He got out of bed and stumbled to the window. The garden was as green as ever. There wasn't a single trace of snow.

They raced downstairs and sure enough there were presents lying by the chimney and sweets scattered over the floor. Luke went over to the window and stood there staring. Laya rushed to her shoe. "Look Mum, he didn't want your phone!" She held it high. "He didn't want a holiday either. He chose the chocolate." Their mother shot a warning glance at Luke, afraid he was going to make one of his usual remarks, but to her great surprise he didn't say a thing.

She smiled at him and he beamed back. It felt good, as if they were sharing something that Laya didn't know about. But what it exactly was, Luke couldn't rightly say.

S. R. Harris

Sarah R. Harris lives in Belgium and Scotland and her children's books have been translated into Dutch and French. She writes newspaper articles, runs writing workshops in schools and adult education centres and is currently working on an adult novel. Her sheep stories can be found on the website www.asheepcalledskye.com

Before Twilight

It was that time of day before twilight when you can still see the colour of things, although the brightness is dimmed, a time when you might walk in the garden to check the growth of new carrots and wonder at the beauty of the magnolia, walk past the herbs and press a few leaves together to release their smell. It was the time just before the street lights at the end of the lane responded to the low light levels, opened their eyes and lit up the road for the motorists. Drivers need the street lighting so that they can get to where they were going in a hurry, she thought, but they miss so much. They miss the fading of the day, and the pleasure in that. It was early spring, before the clocks were moved forward to give the extra light in the evening. The weather was mild and the smell of freshness was in the air. All the people who lived in the village and worked a regular day had returned home by now, even those who worked in town, and so there was little traffic on the road as Betty left the house and walked towards the village.

They had had an early supper. She had cleared away and washed up while her husband sat in his chair in front of the television. He watched a lot of television since he'd retired, but still said it was a waste of time. She had put on her anorak, changed into comfortable walking shoes, taken her bag and left. She told George she was going but she did not expect that he had heard her. There was some sporting event on television.

It took about half an hour to walk to the village. George always took the car, but she preferred to walk, especially if she was in no hurry. It allowed her to look at her surrounding again, to note changes in the crops, in people's gardens, to note the houses for sale. She liked to know what was happening in the village they had chosen for their lazy days, even though she was leaving. She hitched her bag onto her shoulders. It was more like a small backpack than a conventional handbag, and George had never liked it.

In the village, she got into the bus going to town and waited for its departure. There were only three other people on the bus, two whispering teenagers and an old man. She wondered how they could afford to keep it running with so few passengers. Another seven boarded the bus before it arrived in the market square, but it still felt empty. She walked from the bus station to the train, and got onto her sleeper for London.

George watched the telly all evening. The football match was succeeded by the news and Panorama. He must have dozed off after that, because it was past midnight when he realised that he was thirsty and also needed the bathroom. Betty usually made him a drink before she went up to bed. What was she thinking of? He poured himself a whisky instead and drank it in his own good time before going upstairs. Betty would be lying there, pretending to be asleep as usual.

He cleaned his teeth, humming loudly, walked into their bedroom and stopped. There was no-one in the bed. He checked his watch. It was nearly one o'clock in the morning. He went back into the bathroom. He checked the spare room. He went downstairs again and checked the living room, the kitchen, the pantry and the cloakroom. He was sober now. In the back of his mind he knew this searching was pointless, but he had to be sure. He took the torch and searched the garden, the shed and the green-house. He came back inside and sat down. His heart was pounding and his stomach knotted. He did not want to think about what might have happened. Suddenly he was furious. What was she playing at?

He didn't know what was happening, but mostly he didn't know what to do. Betty was the one who always suggested what they should do. She was usually wrong, but her suggestions prompted him. Like the time when the car broke down on the motorway and she wanted to walk back to the last service station. Stupid woman. With all that traffic. She could have been killed! He would have fixed it himself if the Police patrol hadn't come along and insisted that they get towed off to the garage. She didn't like cars.

Where the hell was she?

He didn't want to call the police. She might be with friends. When had he last seen her? They'd had supper at 6.30. Or was it a bit later? He couldn't be sure. He remembered her saying something. Goodbye? Perhaps she'd gone visiting. There was a woman in the village called Sarah, Sally, something like that. They went to garden shows together. But not in the middle of the night. He'd leave things until the morning.

He went upstairs again and sat on the bed and started to take off his slippers. They were wet.

How would it look if he didn't report her missing? If he just went to sleep with his wife unaccounted for? On the other hand, if she'd said she was staying with this Sarah for some reason, he'd look a fool if he alerted the police. It was too late to ring the woman now. He'd have to wait until morning. Bloody women. Why didn't she say she'd be staying with a friend? Though why she wanted to be away all night, at her age, he couldn't fathom. She was better off at home.

He didn't sleep well and woke with a feeling of unease. He found Sarah Browning's number and phoned her before he went downstairs. She was surprised by the call:

it was not yet 7.00 a.m. and she had never spoken to him before. She had no idea where Betty was. He put the phone down before she could start pestering him with questions and rang 999. A voice asked which service he wanted and, as he answered "Police", he realised there could have been an accident. The shock of that possibility made him stutter and make a fool of himself when the voice on the phone asked for his name. The police were polite but not much help. They asked all the questions he had already asked himself, including the one about accidents. They confirmed that they had had no reports concerning a Mrs Betty Sullivan and said they would check the hospitals.

They rang back midmorning with nothing to report and a reassuring, condescending voice said that, in cases like this, the missing person usually turned up within a couple of days and so not to worry. What a stupid thing to say. He hadn't been able to eat any breakfast. He didn't know what to do. He wasn't going to just wait around until his stupid wife chose to turn up.

He stormed out of the house, got in his car and drove down to the village. He parked by the sub-post office, walked in and stood at the counter. What now?

"My wife been in this morning?" he barked.

"Sorry, Mr Sullivan, haven't seen Betty since last week. She forgotten something then?"

He snorted, walked out and headed for the paper-shop, but stopped. He didn't want those people in there asking stupid questions as well. Not their business. Somebody walked past and greeted him. He looked up startled. Couldn't stand here all day. He turned and walked over to the pub and took his whiskey into the usual corner.

"Starting early today, Mr Sullivan?" the barman had said, but he ignored him. Perhaps it was the lack of food, or perhaps it was the knowledge that no-body was waiting for him with dinner in the oven, or maybe, just maybe it was a sense of loss that led to his sixth whiskey, his tumble onto the floor in a stupor, his transportation home by the landlord's son and hence the discovery by the whole village that his wife had left him.

Sarah was the only one who took pity on him. She had only known him as her friend's irascible husband who acted like an ex-army major, though she knew he had only ever worked in an office in town. They had not been friends long, but Betty had poured out her grievances, blaming him for the dullness of their retirement. She had tried to be helpful and had pointed out that there must be a strong bond between them if their marriage had lasted this long, but Betty was not mollified. She was adamant that he had become an impossible martinet and that all the strong, honourable qualities that she had loved when they were young had atrophied, making him a tyrant who expected to be waited on hand and foot , who mocked all her ideas and picked holes in her plans. Betty had always wanted to travel, to break out of her conventional lifestyle, to have adventures. She had hoped to persuade George to take her on exotic cruises, a trip to India at least, once they had the time. He had refused. He didn't like travelling. They were quite alright as they were. He expected her to be content with her new kitchen! She had felt more and more stifled. Sarah was not surprised that she had left, only the manner of her leaving, without a word to anyone and no forwarding address. A clean break.

George resented Sarah's nosiness at first. Of course he was alright. Or course he could manage. Did the woman think he was a child who needed to be looked after? He had his lunch at the pub and made sorties to the freezer in the village store. He couldn't see why Betty had needed to traipse all the way into town for food. It hadn't taken him long to get into a routine, and when things broke, he replaced them. The garden was looking scruffy though. He asked in the pub, but couldn't find a gardener. He found himself getting out the lawn mower when the grass got too long, but it wouldn't start. They were more interested when he mentioned that in the pub. Everybody wanted to give him advice about engines, but it was Ron, the barman, who eventually got it going. He had walked back to the bungalow with him one afternoon, primed it and it started at once. He guessed that George had flooded the engine. George was delighted and mowed the whole lawn at once. Then he had the pleasure of giving the barman a beer in his own house. The two of them sat back in contentment, smelling the grass.

After that he began to enjoy the results of his labour. He started tidying up the edges and snipping off the dead heads. You could get used to being out here, he thought on a day when the sun was shining and the breeze from the west was making the long grass in the field change colour as it swayed. A bench here at the bottom, by the apple tree, would be nice, he thought. He'd see about getting one. Soon he noticed men cutting, then baling the tall grass with its coppery red tops. They said it was for silage, when he asked in the pub. They said there'd be cows in the field soon. Strange, he'd never noticed cows in the field. He must ask Betty if they'd always had cows in the field.

Suddenly, as if someone had hit him in the belly, he collapsed onto his knees on the lawn and started to whimper. He wanted to howl, but he couldn't. He wanted Betty. He wanted his wife, he wanted to see her, to hear her voice, to show her how he was looking after her garden.

Almost as quickly, he regained control. It was stupid to want what you can't have. She'd chosen to leave and he could manage fine without her. He turned to look at the lane. No-one had seen his unseemly display. He mopped his brow. And his eyes. He went back into the house.

Sarah had been about to come to his aid after seeing him kneeling on the grass. Over the summer she had grown to respect the man: he had got on with his life and had never been heard to complain about his wife's departure. He never spoke of her at all. It had worried Sarah. That morning when she received the letter, she had resolved to come and see him and to talk about Betty. She hurried to the gate and was about to open it when she recognised the heaving of his shoulders as grief. It was not the time to tell him about Betty's letter, which said she was having a great time, but which had twice asked how George was. Sarah turned away and wrote back that same evening.

The clocks had gone back when the evening bus returned to the village with its handful of passengers and Betty got off and began the walk back home, still in her sensible shoes with her small backpack. She walked slowly perhaps because she was she was savouring the autumn smells and checking the crops and the neighbours gardens. The street lights were on, but they were not yet noticed as the sunset was strong.

She stopped at the sound of the lawn mower, put her backpack by the gate and walked into the garden. George was mowing the lawn and whistling. He used to whistle, when she first knew him, and she had said it sounded common, so he had stopped. The memory made her shudder: had she really been so intolerant and pettish. She started to cry, turning her face to the wall and crying for all the times when they had been close and all the times when they had pushed one another away.

He didn't call her name, but touched her very gently on the shoulder and whispered "Betty?" with such hope in his voice that all her fears were gone. She took his hand and turned to face him.

"Yes" she said. This was her George and she was his Betty and they looked at one another for a long time.

Jean Lyon

Jean Lyon lives within sight of Snowdonia. She has published academic work, but now writes poetry, short stories and has the first draft of a novel. e-mail: jeanlyon@btinternet.com

Mantek's Journey

Charlek was lying amongst the horses' straw. His face was grey, his lips blue. I knelt down beside him. I could feel his breath on my cheek. Prince, the Master's latest stallion, was pawing nervously at the ground.

Charlek stirred a little. He grabbed my tunic and pulled me towards him, until my ear was level with his mouth.

"You must … you must," he struggled to say. "You must go with the Master. To where the star is taking him." He made the sign of blessing on my forehead. He took in a long rasping breath. His chest rattled and then he was silent.

"Is he… is he ?" asked Zarib.

I nodded. I had seen a man die once before. My father, too, had collapsed just like that.

So, I was now to be in charge of the stable boys and oversee the grooming of the Master's fine horses. I was secretly pleased. Not that Charlek had died, you understand – he had been a good friend – but that I could take on this new responsibility. I had dreamt for a long time of being in charge of a stable. I was capable of the task, too. I was fond of Charlek. But his death had at least saved me seeking a new position.

We carried Charlek to his final resting place on a cool clear day. The Master attended but said very little. He did not join in our singing and dancing at the wake. Before he went back to his quarters, he drew me aside.

"Come to me when the celebration is over," he said.

I went to him that evening. I had never been so close to the Master before. He normally preferred his own company. He had no wife and no children and was never seen with a companion. I gawped at how much taller and younger he looked close to. His beard must have made him seem older before.

I had never been to his rooms. They were like nothing I had ever seen. The walls were covered in blue and red silks. There were thick mats on the floor and the room was furnished with soft chairs and sofas. The Master himself was also clothed in fine silks and satins.

He was looking out of the window through a long tube when I came in. He must have heard me, for he spoke though he did not turn to look at me.

"Mantek. Good, you are here," he said. "We are to go on a journey." He still looked out of the window and not directly at me. "Does that suit you Mantek?"

I did not know what to say. I had just taken charge of the stable. I did not want to leave. I wanted to prove I could run everything as well as Charlek had, if not better.

"You are very quiet, Mantek," he said. "Does the idea of travelling not please you?"

I still could not speak.

Then he turned to me. "Come," he said, gesturing that I should join him at the window. He pointed towards the sky. "Do you see that star? The one in the East? Brighter than the rest?"

I looked to where he was pointing. I did not know much about the stars, but I could see that this one was shining more brightly than those around it.

"It is a new star," the Master continued. "We have been waiting for it for hundreds of years."

Now he looked deeply into my eyes.

"Only three of us will go," he said. "I shall take only two men I can trust. You are one of those men, Mantek. I know you will look after my horses well. Now go, and prepare yourself and six fine horses for the journey. "

I was flattered. Not many fifteen year-olds are spoken to as equals by men older than them, let alone by someone as wise and as rich as our Master. But that did not stop me feeling worried about the journey. Good as I was with the horses, I wasn't sure I could look after them properly away from the comfortable stable. And I was sure that all too soon the Master would find out I was no more than a boy when my competence or my courage, or both, failed.

Two days later we set off at dusk. The star shone brightly even then. We planned to travel mainly by night, so that we could always see the star. I believe it was actually so bright we would have still been able to see it during the day.

All went well at first. I was pleased that I had chosen the right horses. Each day we rode three and three carried our extra supplies. Archamid, the longest-serving of the Master's other servants, accompanied us. The horses were well-behaved and strong. We made good progress, though I was not sure exactly where we were going. The Master talked to Archamid as though he were a friend and not a servant at all. They said little to me, and I was left to my own thoughts. But they didn't treat me like a boy and they showed me every respect when they wanted to know about the animals. I was the expert then. I was allowed to do everything for the horses on my own. Except that the master always insisted in packing his own things. Every evening, I saw him place very carefully into his saddlebag. something wrapped in several pieces of cloth

We slept by day. It was warm then and we could get snug in our tents. I was much better cared for there than I was at home: the stable master always sleeps in the stables with the horses. Here, the horses were kept outside the tents and my tent was as fine as those of Archamid's and the Master's.

But on the third evening the trouble began.

Archamid was frowning.

"This sand gets everywhere," he said, shaking some from out of his boot. "We shall look like tramps by the time we find what the star wants to show us." He complained all the time. It was too cold. The saddle was making him sore. He had no idea where we were going.

The Master said nothing but continued to stare at the star.

By the fourth evening Archamid was even more restless.

"I'm too old for this sort of journey," he complained. "I should be resting in the comfort of my own little home at my age." For the rest of that night there were even more moans and groans from him.

Still the Master said nothing. I wanted to argue with Archamid, and tell him he was being selfish, but my Master's solemn silence would not let me.

On the fifth evening, just as the sun was getting low in the sky and we were loading the horses ready to leave, Archamid started again.

"What will we do when we find the star's final resting place?" he asked. "Will we find riches there, fit to bring back to our families?"

"There will be no treasure that you will recognise," said the Master softly.

"What?" cried Archamid. "You are dragging us away from our homes? And there will be no return?" His face was red with anger.

"What you find there will be greater than treasure but you will not be able to pick it up and carry it," said the Master, again speaking calmly.

"You are fooling me," said Archamid.

The Master smacked Tangent's rump hard.

The fine horse bolted, along with Archamid's belongings.

I wanted to gallop out and retrieve the animal. I mounted Starcrest, his brother, ready to follow. The Master stopped me with the wave of his arm.

"You go and retrieve your belongings," said the Master to Archamid, "as material goods are so important to you."

Archamid jumped on Snow and followed Tangent. We watched them disappear into the distance.

"They will not be back," said the Master. "They are lost to us forever, and I fear that Archamid has lost himself, too, and it will be difficult for him to find the right path again. But you will continue on the journey with me?" he asked.

I nodded. Two of my good horses were lost. I must stay with the other four. "How much longer will it take?" I asked.

The Master looked up at the sky for a few minutes.

"Ten more days, I think," he said.

I too looked at the star. It was even brighter and bigger than before. I thought it might explode.

We travelled on. The Master did not say much. I occupied myself with the four remaining horses. They covered the miles well. We became used to just following the star. I soon learnt to forget the noises of the day. I relished each dawn the softness of my feather mattress and the comfort of the smooth silk sheets pulled over me. It was easy, really, to sleep in the heat in our cool tents. I always took care to find shade for the horses too.

On the thirteenth night, the star seemed even closer and brighter. The Master stared at it constantly and seemed in a trance. I wondered whether it might be the gentle movement of the horses which had lulled him into his dream state. But I did not feel rocked to sleep. I was wide awake with the stirrings of some great expectation. I had no idea what was to happen, but I sensed the importance of these times.

The sun came slowly up. We made camp as usual. I tied the horses and gave them food and water. The supplies were dwindling, but the Master assured me we would be able to find enough at our destination for the return journey. I gave the animals their full ration and then started to cook a meal for the Master and myself.

"Mantek!" the Master called suddenly. "Listen."

I heard nothing at first. Then there was a sound. A rustling amongst the trees.

"Take up arms!" shouted the Master.

Two men appeared from the nearby bushes. They had shining swords. I had no weapon on me and although the Master wore a sword, he made no attempt to use it. The rough-looking men jumped at him. He moved his right arm quickly and the taller of the two men bowled over, as if struck by a hard rock. The second charged at the Master who raised his staff which seemed to almost decapitate the shorter of the two men. He let out a piercing cry. The Master looked white with fury. The second rushed forward again, but the Master repelled him as well with the staff. The would-be thief hurtled into our water jug. There was a loud crack. The last of our water trickled on to the sandy ground and disappeared at once. The two men, shaken and bruised, crawled away, muttering curses at my Master. We were safe. But we had no water.

"Do you think we shall hold out?" I asked. "Can we really go any further without water?"

"We have just two more days' sleep and two more nights" to travel," replied the Master. "The Power of the Star will protect us for this time."

He seemed to believe what he was saying. But I was doubtful. The day-time heat became too fierce as we travelled eastwards and though it was much cooler at night, our bodies needed fluids.

We slept for the rest of that day. The next evening when I saddled the horses, I worried about their lack of water.

"Please forgive me," I whispered to Stardust and Prince, to Chaser and Gallant. "There is no water tonight." I'm not sure what those dumb animals thought, but they seemed to appreciate me talking to them. Prince nuzzled my face and all four neighed softly.

At first it was not too bad. We made good progress and I did not feel thirsty. The star shimmered and glistened before us. It carried on becoming brighter and bigger as it had every night. Now, the whole of the Eastern sky was alight.

Then, just before day break, there came a change, however, and I do not know to this day whether it was the lack of water making me hallucinate or whether the whole sky really was filled with men-like creatures that had great feathered wings. They seemed to be made of light. There was sound. Voice music, such as I had never heard before and have never heard since. The Master seemed to move in slow motion. He mouthed something to me, but I could not make out what he said.

I don't remember stopping to sleep. I do remember waking the next evening. The Master was shaking me.

"Mantek," he said – I could hear him now, for he was very close to me – "Are you going to sleep all night? Do you not want to see the King's glory?"

We continued through the last night. The sky was still ablaze with light. I could still hear the singing, but could no longer make out the shapes of the men with

240

wings. There was just light, more and more light. We arrived at a small town. The Master spoke to a woman. They seemed to talk for a long time, and she did not look best pleased. Eventually, she led us to a well. We drank. Then, I filled a trough for the horses. They weren't as thirsty as I expected, though they did make noises which I thought told me they were glad of the water. The sun would soon be up. The light faded from the sky, leaving the star shining brilliantly against a now dark sky. It seemed to point to a low building, a stable perhaps. How odd. Hadn't the Master said something about a King?

He spoke again to the woman – I couldn't understand what they said – the people there did not speak our language. She pointed towards the building over which the star shone.

Strangely, the horses seemed to know what to do. With no command from me, they moved steadily towards the building which looked less and less like the home of a King the nearer we got to it. I did not trust the woman. I thought she was out to trick us and that we would once again be attacked by thieves – maybe her brothers.

But more and more people were making their way to the same place. If we were being tricked, we weren't the only ones. The Master seemed to know all the other travellers. Some rode on camels, others on horses, and some as fine as our own, some less so. They all appeared to be bringing gifts, – fine linens, spices, ointments. At last the Master took out what he had kept so closely guarded in Prince's saddle-bag – a large nugget of the purest gold.

We all moved silently. We did not speak as we approached the birth place of the King. But later, after we had seen the babe, my Master conversed for hours with the other Sages and Wiseman. Again I could not understand what they said but I could tell they were excited to exchange their wisdom about the event.

In the stable we found an ordinary woman and her man, and the baby. He had no crib, nor fine clothes fit for a king. He had no servant, just this older man who I could not believe was His father. But I don't think I have ever seen such a serene child or such a radiant mother. The light which shone from their faces was brighter even than that of the star and of whatever else I saw in the skies above. This child was a bringer of peace. That much was clear. I just knew it, even though no one told me. Tiny baby that he was, his eyes held mine for a split second and I know he could see right into me, and he understood everything about me. Understood, me yes, – and this is going to sound a bit crazy – no very crazy – he forgave me for the mistakes I've made. Now, he only looked at me for a few seconds, but we understood each other in that time, me and him.

And here were all these wise men, kings in their own right, bowing down before Him. We all knew He was going to bring peace to this world. How, I could not imagine, especially from this small place, but as soon as I looked at Him, all desire left me and I felt only deep contentment.

On the way out of the town we met the woman who had taken us to the well and shown us the way to the stable. She spoke for a few minutes to my Master.

"Do you know that woman used to be a prostitute?" said the Master after we'd waved good-bye to her. "That's why she was wary of us – she thinks all men want only one thing. But she's just told me she will never go back on the game. One look from that Holy Child was enough."

Just as one look, just as it had been for me. It didn't last forever, of course. The rest of my life has not been without its ups and downs, and there has been plenty of agitation with a wife and five daughters to feed and tolerate. But I often think back to the time we followed the star and then I am filled with a delightful calm.

On the way home, the Master told me of the great prophecy that said a Prince of Peace would be born under that star. We've heard a little of that Holy Child since. He too has become a man and he performs miracles and tells the priests in His country their business. We had a miracle, I think, on the way home. Our horses travelled lightly. We took five days less to get home than we had taken to go there. We ran out of neither grain nor water. Nor did we meet any thieves.

I think I was meant to see that child. God forgive me, but I think that's why Charlek had his heart attack. He went in peace and I think he knew. That's why he gave me his blessing.

Gill James

Gill James writes mainly for children and young adults, fiction and non-fiction. She is a lecturer in Creative Writing at the University of Salford. She enjoys finding the extraordinary behind the ordinary. www.gilljames.co.uk

Index of Authors

A.J. Humphrey, 47

Annie Bates, 95

Debz Hobbs-Wyatt, 22

Gill James, 243

Ian Charles Douglas, 39

Jean Lyon, 233

Jenny Robertson, 65

Joyce Hicks, 130

Linda Lewis, 58, 146, 167, 193

Michael O'Connor, 139

Noreen Wainwright, 122

Nurgish Watkins, 115

Oscar Peebles, 160

Phillip Dean Thomas, 108

Rebecca Holmes, 82

Rosemary A. Bach-Holzer, 218

Rosemary Gemmell, 72

Sally Angell, 31

Sarah R. Harris, 225

Wendy Busby, 203

Yvonne Eve Walus, 182

Printed in the United Kingdom
by Lightning Source UK Ltd.
134929UK00001B/61-108/P